ZOMBIE TALES

NOW AVAILABLE AND COMING SOON FROM UNDEAD PRESS

DEADLY HUNT: A ZOMBIE SURVIVAL STORY
CAVALCADE OF TERROR

ZOMBIE TALES

EDITED BY
VINCENZO BILOF
AND
ANTHONY GIANGREGORIO

Table of Contents

THE TWITCHY THINGS

ROCKY ALEXANDER

The little girl pressed her shaking hands over her ears to muffle the awful screams emanating from the woman outside. Her uncle, Eric—whose voice betrayed a fear at least as great as her own—kept saying, "It's okay, Melissa," over and over again.

But Melissa knew it wasn't okay. Things would never be *okay* again.

Her mother had always told her there was no such thing as monsters, but her daddy had said that monsters do, in fact, exist in the world. He'd taught her about monsters named Dahmer, Bundy, Gacy, and others, but for some reason Daddy never thought to warn her of the twitchy things which had been appearing on the streets in growing numbers over the past hour or so.

Through the window of her uncle's small, suburban house, Melissa had watched the things come and go—sometimes one at a time, sometimes two or more together—shambling along like the drunken beggars she occasionally observed in the city. Although the creatures were anatomically the same as people and dressed in varied styles of clothing, they were nonetheless unmistakably *non-human.*

Their movements were graceless and spasmodic—*twitchy*, as if somehow affected by a high-voltage electrical current. Some of them had ashen skin that was marked by dark bruises. A good many of the things had quite clearly gone to the bathroom in their pants, and a few were covered in what appeared to be blood. At one point, the man who lived across the street came outside to try to talk to a couple of the things, but they forced him to the ground and held him there while they tore open his neck and belly with their teeth.

That's when Melissa's terror became a tangible entity which threatened to swallow her whole. Once she'd starting screaming, she didn't think she would ever be able to stop.

Eric, who had been transfixed by the special news bulletin on television warning people to stay indoors because of some bizarre outbreak, had shot out of his chair at the sound of Melissa wailing hysterically in another room. He'd found the child at the dining room window, looking out at Cheryl, the neighbor across the street, striking some man repeatedly on the head with a golf club as he continued to lumber toward her, apparently undeterred by the smashing blows. On the lawn, only a few feet away, lay another man on his back, his organs visible through the large, ragged hole in his abdomen. Eric recognized the face of the man as Cheryl's husband, Donnie. A third man, on his hands and knees, thrust his mouth directly into Donnie's exposed organs and began...*eating*? The first man finally managed to grab Cheryl by her forearm and pulled her, thrashing and screaming, into a crushing bear hug, then sank his teeth into her throat. Cheryl's blood-curdling shrieks quickly waned, and her body convulsed for a few seconds before going limp in the man's grip.

Eric watched it all in complete horror and disbelief. He felt frozen in place, as if his feet were encased in concrete. Melissa had dropped to the floor and now sat with her back to the wall beneath the window frame, sobbing uncontrollably. She begged her uncle— or God, *someone*—to make the monsters go away, but at that moment, Eric was helpless to do anything but watch. He heard an alien voice reverberating in his ears, and realized it was his own.

"It's okay, Melissa... It's okay, Melissa... It's okay, Melissa..."

More of the things were beginning to accumulate on the lawn across the street, all undoubtedly seeking a share of what was left of Donnie and Cheryl. More screaming could be heard from both men and women from further down the block. A car alarm blared from somewhere in the distance. Police sirens howled from too far away to matter. The world began to oscillate, and Eric turned and vomited on the dining room floor.

When he returned his attention to the scene outside, he looked straight into the eyes of the man who now stood on the sidewalk in front of the house. Eric willed himself to snatch Melissa up and away from the window, as the man rushed forward and began pounding on the glass with the palms of his hands.

"Please, sir, let me in! Help me, *please!*"

Eric's heart was hammering so rapidly in his chest he felt it might explode. He opened his mouth to shout at the man to go away, but the only sound he could extract from his vocal cords was a pathetic whimper. Across the street, Donnie–minus most of his internal organs and a good portion of his flesh–rose from the lawn and lumbered toward the desperate man who continued to pound on Eric's window. The other things–Eric counted six of them out there now–had apparently heard the man's frenzied pleas, because they too had begun to move in his direction. Eric stepped cautiously toward the quarter-inch thick glass which separated him and his seven-year-old niece from the nightmarish world outside, his quivering lips repeatedly forming a single, silent word:

"*Run.*"

The panic-stricken guy on the other side of the window finally backed away, took a quick look around at the foul, undead things closing in on his position, and sprinted off down the street as swiftly as his legs would carry him. Four of the creatures attempted to pursue him, but the remaining three were now focused on Eric and the little girl. There was one new addition as well: a zombie-thing which differed from the others in that it walked *backwards*, most likely due to the fact that, with the connective tissue of its neck having been eaten away almost completely, its head dangled lifelessly between its shoulder blades. Its eyes could only see *behind* its bloody mess of a body.

It was Cheryl.

Melissa felt shameful of her fear. Big girls don't cry–her daddy had told her that—but she had never before in her life experienced anything so frightening. She'd screamed so loudly for so long that her throat burned and her head throbbed with pain. Her face was wet with salty tears that stung her eyes. She wished for her mommy and daddy to come and take her far, far away from the twitchy things outside, but she knew they wouldn't come, because they'd already gone to Heaven after the car crash nearly a year ago. Uncle Eric held her tightly in his strong arms and stroked her hair, but it wasn't enough to take her fear away.

She wanted to scream again when she saw the monsters staggering toward the window, but her voice was stifled from the agonizing soreness in her throat. Eric purposefully carried her into the living room, where he grabbed his cell phone and car keys off a table beside the sofa, then hurried to the door in the kitchen which opened into the adjacent garage where his car was parked. Melissa heard glass breaking in the dining room—the twitchy things were trying to get in.

Once she and her uncle were safely buckled in the car with the engine running, Eric hit the button on the automatic garage door remote. The door opened to reveal *the-thing-that-used-to-be-Cheryl* standing in the middle of the driveway. Eric hesitated only for a second before shifting the transmission into reverse and stomping on the gas pedal. Tires squealed on the concrete floor as the Ford Mustang rocketed backward into the driveway, striking Cheryl with a satisfying *thump*! Melissa watched the head separate from its body before bouncing off the rear windshield and flying onto the asphalt. The body fell beneath the vehicle and was crushed to a mangled mess of meat and bone as Eric drove over it.

Upon exiting the driveway, Eric threw the shifter into first gear and floored the accelerator once more. As they sped through the neighborhood, Melissa saw twitchy things attempting to break into a number of homes on both sides of the street. She felt sorry for the people inside. There were more of the creatures staggering across lawns and along the sidewalks. A few stumbled around in the road. They made no effort to get out of the way of the Mustang as it hurtled toward them at sixty miles per hour, the engine roaring. Eric swerved to miss them, but one was struck in the lower body by the front bumper and went tumbling like a bowling pin.

At one point, Melissa noticed a little blonde-haired girl in a blue dress standing by a mailbox.

"Uncle Eric, it's *Samantha*!"

Melissa had met Samantha only a few days after moving in with Uncle Eric. The two had been the best of friends ever since. They had spent many afternoons playing together at each other's homes after school, and Melissa had even slept over at Samantha's house on a number of occasions. Their close friendship had made it appreciably easier for Melissa to deal with the death of her parents.

As the Mustang slowed, Melissa could see that Samantha's dress was torn and dirty. There was blood on the little girl's right arm. Her skin was waxy and pale, and there was a distinct blankness in her eyes. Her legs wobbled as she moved toward the car.

Samantha was a twitchy thing now.

Eric placed a reassuring hand on Melissa's shoulder as he stepped on the gas. "Close your eyes, honey. Don't look."

Melissa's sorrow was like a huge weight pressing against her from all sides. She brought her knees up to her chest and wept.

Eric, in his blind determination to get himself and his niece to safety—if there was such a thing anymore—drove as fast as he dared, tearing through intersections, fish-tailing around corners, and dodging the walking—or sometimes *crawling*—dead men, women, and children that sporadically wandered into his path. It wasn't long before he was on the main road leading to the inter-state. He would feel safer once he was doing about a hundred on the freeway, but he had a few miles to go before he reached the entrance ramp. There were other vehicles on the road as well, all of them speeding along in the same direction as he—away.

There were numerous fires burning. Every so often Eric would pass a home, business, or vehicle that was engulfed in flames. Thick clouds of oily, black smoke drifted across the sky. In the parking lot of a blazing warehouse, Eric saw human forms on fire, their bodies contorting and arms flailing wildly as they burned. He couldn't tell whether they were live people or the living dead. The scene caused him to shudder.

When he finally spotted the freeway entrance ramp, which was still three long blocks ahead of them, Eric was overcome with an excited sense of triumph. He glanced over at Melissa, still curled into a fetal position in the passenger seat, and gently touched the back of her head.

"We're going to make it, Baby Girl. We're going to be okay."

On the left side of the street, a man-thing and a woman-thing were on their hands and knees, their teeth tearing away chunks of some poor soul who was laying face-down on the sidewalk.

Two blocks to go.

Eric could hear the swell of a police siren close by. He could see cars and trucks racing across the overpass ahead.

One block...

"Uncle Eric, look out!"

The last thing Eric saw were the flashing red and blue strobes atop the police car that smashed into the driver's side door of his Mustang.

The impact caused the car to become airborne momentarily before careening across the intersection and plowing head-on into the exterior wall of a corner liquor store. When it was over, Melissa wiggled her fingers to see if she still could, then carefully removed her seat belt so she could try to wake Uncle Eric, who was slumped crookedly in the driver's seat. As she moved, she felt varying degrees of pain throughout her body. Her left knee hurt the most, and she worried that she may have broken her leg. She crawled closer to Eric and gave him a vigorous shake as she called his name, but he wouldn't wake up. When she saw that he wasn't breathing, she began to sob in despair.

From behind her, Melissa heard what sounded like cats moaning in the distance. When she turned and looked through the shattered passenger-side window, she could see that the eerie sounds were in fact coming from the two twitchy things that had been eating a man down the street just a few yards away from her. Chunks of flesh trickled from between their blood-stained teeth as they turned their attention to her.

With their vacant, unblinking eyes focused on the desperate girl, the twitchy things dragged their feet across the cement. Following closely behind them was the man they'd voraciously devoured. The fresh corpse spilled the remaining contents of its exposed stomach—two organs plopped near its slow-moving feet, splashing blood along the concrete and across the creature's pant legs.

In utter desperation, Melissa began to shake her uncle once again. "Uncle Eric, please wake up. WAKE UP!"

But Uncle Eric was gone. Melissa was alone and the twitchy things were coming for her—they were getting closer. She made a fierce effort to open her car door and escape, but the door was stuck. Their shadows fell upon her in the glare of the still-roving strobes atop the damaged police car nearby. She flung herself over the top of the door and came down on her injured leg. She squealed in horror and pain as the monsters closed in. She tried to scurry away but the man-thing grabbed her by the ankle. Then the woman-thing was there, reaching for her. Melissa closed her eyes and screamed.

Suddenly, there was a deafening *BOOM* and the twitchy woman fell on top of her. When Melissa opened her eyes, she saw that the monster's head was gone. There was another thunderous booming sound and the man-thing's face exploded. Its body toppled backwards onto the ground. Two more booms and the third twitchy thing dropped as well.

Melissa lay beneath the headless corpse of the woman-thing for several seconds, too scared to even breathe. Through the blurry haze of tears she could see a limping figure approaching. It made a scraping noise as it dragged one foot across the asphalt. A soft groan escaped its throat as it reached for her.

Everything went black.

Melissa awoke in a windowless room illuminated only by the harsh glow of a single flashlight. Around her were crates of bottled liquor, beer kegs, stacks of cigarette cartons, and a variety of other boxed goods. Beside her sat a man dressed in a tan police uniform. There was blood on his head, and he cradled a shotgun in one arm. Static-filled voices conversed over the portable radio on his belt. Melissa couldn't make sense of what they were saying.

"Are you a twitchy thing?"

He stared down at her quizzically. "What?"

Melissa felt relief after hearing the man speak. "You aren't one of them. I can tell."

"I'm a policeman, sweetie. I'm here to protect you. My name's Officer Mike. What's yours?"

"Melissa."

"It's very nice to meet you, Melissa." He offered a hand and she gave it a cautious shake.

"How'd I get here?"

The officer moved closer to her and spoke sweetly. "I found you outside on the street. I brought you into the store to wait with me until the other policemen can get here to pick us up."

Melissa looked up with a spark of hope in her eyes. "How long will it be before the other policemen come?"

"They're coming now." Mike's words followed the rhythmic beat of helicopter blades outside. "You ever take a ride on a helicopter before?"

Melissa shook her head.

"Well, you're gonna love it. It's a lot of fun."

A voice on the radio said, "Four-Eleven, we have your vehicle in sight. What is your twenty?"

Officer Mike spoke into a microphone which was tethered to his radio by a coiled black cord. "I'm in a storage room at the back of the liquor store on the corner." He paused for a moment. "The building with the wrecked Ford Mustang and three dead zombies out front. I have a survivor with me—a little girl. My ankle is messed up pretty badly. I can't walk too well."

"Copy that, Four-Eleven. We're arriving now. Standby."

Mike looked down at the little girl on the storeroom floor with her cuts and bruises and weary eyes. He couldn't begin to fathom what she'd been through. He put his arm around her shoulders and held her close. "It's over, sweetie. You're safe now."

Melissa considered those words: *It's over*. She wanted to believe it, she really did. But deep inside she knew it was only the beginning.

BLIND

ALYN DAY

You're startled awake suddenly from a deep sleep. There's a loud crash from outside. You hear Mary groaning, as she groggily pulls herself from sleep in the other room. There's another crash followed by a loud thud. Something slaps against the door down the hall with a wet, fleshy sound. There's a low, mournful moan coming from somewhere nearby. You can't see, but it's nothing new. You've been like this from birth.

The sound of glass shattering fills the air. You hear Mary frantically moving in the other room, and the faint sound of three buttons being pushed on the phone in rapid succession. Mary mutters angrily under her breath, then the clatter of the phone dropping to the floor.

More crashes from outside. You hear the wind whistling. Is a window broken? you wonder. Your heart beat is thundering in your ears so loudly that for a moment you think it's coming from somewhere else, another of those strange sounds that erupted out of the night.

Something heavy falls to the floor in the living room with a jarring thud. Mary's door opens. "Hello? Is someone there? I'm warning you, I have a gun!" Mary's voice falters. You know she doesn't have a gun. You don't think she has ever even touched one and you're sure she wouldn't know how to use it if she did. Mary couldn't hurt a fly.

Soft footsteps come from down the hall. Mary is coming to get you. Relief floods you, warming you like hot chocolate. Mary knows what's going on. She'll make everything all right.

You hear her turn the doorknob slowly, gently. It clicks open and you hear her breathing heavily. Then the sound of the door closing softly behind her, and the click of the lock sliding home. Mary's footsteps on the carpet come towards you, and you detect the sharp tang of sweat. Your bed sags a bit under Mary's weight as she leans on it and you feel her hand on your bare arm. It's hot and slick with moisture.

Mary is breathing very heavily now. She's frightened, which makes you even more scared. Mary is not only your older sister, but also your protector and guardian. If she's scared, then there's a good reason. Fear consumes you and you start to feel a bit sick. Sweat beads on your brow and you can feel yourself shivering. Another loud thud from the hall makes you jump. Closer than the last one, near the end of the hall. There's a faint scent of something, like the meat counter at the Val-U-Mart where Mary takes you to buy groceries sometimes. Then comes the sound of something being dragged along the floor. Mary is pulling you close to her. You can smell the sweat on her, mingling with her Jasmine lotion. She grasps your shoulders so hard that her nails dig in to your skin, hurting you.

"I need you to listen to me, okay?" she whispers, frantic. "I'm going to go out there and see what's going on. I want you to lock the door behind me and stay under the bed until I get back. Don't open the door unless you know it's me, all right?" Frightened, you start to cry. "Okay?" Mary demands, shaking you roughly.

"Okay," is all you can manage to reply.

Mary yanks you out of bed, making you stumble and almost fall. She drags you roughly to the door. "I'm going out there now. But I'll be right back. Remember, don't you open that door for anything!" She hugs you fiercely, almost making it hard to breathe, before she unlocks the door and slips into the hallway, leaving you alone. You lock the door behind her, then lean against it, pressing your ear to the smooth, cool wood.

Soft footsteps moving down the hall. Mary is getting farther away from you. A long, loud moan, dry and deep. Mary whimpers. You press your ear tighter against the door, straining to hear what's going on. A sudden hard thump on the other side makes you jump and fall backwards.

You scoot along the floor until you find the bed and crawl under it. A crash from the living room. More groans. Mary screams. Your heart thuds in your chest so hard it's painful. Footsteps run down the hall. Is it Mary?

She's pounding on the door, frantic. "LET ME IN! OH GOD, OPEN THE FUCKING DOOR!" You've never heard Mary swear before. You scramble out from under the bed and move for the door. More thuds. Mary pounding frantically, screaming louder.

Her screams die in a gurgle just as you reach the door. You hear the sound of something ripping from the other side of the door and the floor under the door is warm and wet. The smell of something coppery mingles with the raw meat smell. You reach for the doorknob, but draw your hand back, hesitating. Is Mary still out there? You're terrified. You can't protect yourself. Mary is all you have and she's banging on the door.

The meat smell intensified, mixed with something like wet garbage. It makes you want to gag. You're frozen, unsure of what to do. More pounding on the door, harder this time. A crack as the door begins to give.

You panic and back up towards your bed, scooting as quickly as you can manage, although you feel rug burn on the back of your legs. You wedge yourself between the bed and the nightstand as the pounding grows louder. The door is breaking!

"Mary?" you call, but there is no answer, only by a chorus of moans. You're crying uncontrollably now, breathing hard and trembling. Your pulse sounds like the ocean in your ears. A heavy thud as the door falls to the floor; a rush of air as it hits the carpet. Something wet slaps against it. Something heavy falls near the doorway.

The meat/garbage smell is overwhelming. You can only sob and press against the wall as rough hands grab you and yank you into the open.

"Mary?" you whimper as sharp fingernails dig into your flesh. You feel breath on your neck, and then an eruption of pain. Warm blood flows down the front of your shirt, mingling with urine as you wet yourself.

The last thing you smell is sweat, blood, and Jasmine lotion.

DEAD CELEBRITIES

JONATHAN TEMPLAR

Donna Marie was still living in the home her husband's fortune had provided. It was the sort of place most people could only hope to catch a glimpse of through sneakily captured aerial shots published in some celebrity lifestyle magazine. Ten bedrooms, two swimming pools, stables, a cinema and a recording studio—it was more like a hotel complex than a single residence.

It proved to be Donna Marie's salvation.

When the 'Event' occurred—that was how the media referred to it now, the 'Event,' hesitant to use the 'Z' word in case it created legal precedence—she'd been at home, miles from civilization, surrounded by a ten foot wall topped with razor wire. Louis had been out in the wide world, surrounded by an army of personal security, his every move monitored and protected. He was supposed to be the safe one. He paid thousands of dollars a day to ensure that safety. But in the security briefings, the prospect of the dead returning to life wasn't considered a viable threat.

When the infection spread, Louis was vulnerable simply *because* he was surrounded. It was a bite from one of his own black-clad retinue that sent the poison into him. He was left dying in a dressing room surrounded by the empty vodka bottles and discarded panties that any serious rock star would be expected to bury themselves in.

Travis felt uncomfortable in Donna Marie's home. He liked to think of himself as a simple man with simple tastes. He had a one bedroom apartment that was sparsely furnished and tamely decorated. Opulence left him bewildered.

So did Donna Marie. He'd seen her lots of times on TV and in the press. After all, he hadn't been living in a cave. She was the wife of a global superstar. But in the flesh, she was different, mostly because she didn't look much like flesh. She seemed to be an animated mannequin with mahogany skin stretched tightly over her bones. Her face didn't move the way a face was supposed to. She had no lines or wrinkles, and at the same time, no depth. It was like looking at a clumsy oil painting.

"You must know what I need from you," she said in a voice intended to sound husky. It didn't.

"I reckon I could probably guess, ma'am."

"Can't you take the fucking glasses off? I know you guys like to create a certain impression, but we're indoors. You look fucking ridiculous."

Travis removed the glasses with an acquiescent nod of the head. He'd kept them on in the hope that they might block out the garish glamour of the palace of poor taste.

"It might be best if you tell me exactly what you'd like me to do for you."

She sat back, long legs curling over each other like a lazy octopus. "You know all about Louis?"

"I do indeed, ma'am."

"He's in that fucking place in Vegas. Twenty four hour performances and someone else is coining all the revenue because he's no longer 'technically' alive. This isn't acceptable to me. Until he's legally dead, I can't make a claim on his life insurance, and trust me, the only reason I put up with the bastard for two decades was the knowledge that one day something he shoved up his nose and someone he shoved on his dick would finally kill him. It was thought kept me company at night, you understand? The thought of him doing the first decent thing since we got married and fucking killing himself."

Travis believed the house was little more than a doll's house built and furnished to keep the plastic bitch amused. He wondered what else she could possibly need or desire, but he nodded his head anyway.

"I want him out of there. I want him to stop fucking moving. Once he's declared legally dead, I can cash in and move on."

"He's going to be well guarded. This is going to be a costly thing to pull off, I'm gonna need help to achieve it. The price is gonna be high."

She sipped top-shelf liquor from a diamond-encrusted glass. "I'll pay all expenses up front. If you can get the fucker in the ground without my fingerprints being anywhere near it, you'll get a twenty percent cut of the insurance money."

Despite any provocation, as Travis was well-practiced in keeping his icy cool veneer, he felt pushed to his outer limit. "That sounds like a fair deal," he said in a neutral voice that didn't betray the excited thoughts exploding behind his eyes like New Year's fireworks. Twenty percent! That would be *millions*. Tens of millions in all likelihood. This would be the last job he would ever need to do. After this, it could be retirement to the Caribbean and cocktails every hour of the day.

"Then you'll do it?" she asked in a voice that sounded close to orgasmic.

Travis allowed a few moments of silence, a last hint of showmanship to make sure that the deal was done. "Reckon I will, ma'am. I'll have your husband dead by Tuesday."

"Wonderful," she purred.

Travis had been hired for a few similar jobs already. Those had been for nobodies, average Joes infected during the Event and forsaken loved ones unable to cash in after the government declared all zombies to be legally alive.

It wasn't as if they really had a choice. The Event had taken everyone by surprise-in a world that was already dipping in and out of recession faster than a randy farmer's dick into a herd of horny sheep—losing fifteen percent of the population in one month was going to have certain consequences. They'd managed to contain the outbreak, securing all the zombies—not that anyone called them that anymore as it suggested a certain *undead* status that the government denied they possessed—and telling the world they were all legally classified as 'transient.' Friends and family had no access to the transient population and no legal right to them under laws that were rewritten daily. They were no longer alive and protected by the old laws, neither were they considered dead. It was all just another shit-storm in a world suddenly full of them.

Of course, the walking corpses of the rich and famous weren't farmed out to internment camps. Not when there was a buck to be made.

Nope. They were all in Vegas.

"Louis *fucking* Starr! Man, I used to love that guy's stuff." Sammy had a grin on his face as wide as the gaps between his brain cells. He was the best in the business at extraction, but if you asked him to read a news headline, he'd flounder.

"Well, I don't imagine he's running through a set of his greatest hits out there in the desert."

"Maybe not, Trav, but hey, this is pretty cool stuff."

Travis sat back in his office chair that was made exclusively for his comfort. He rented this place at a song, used it as somewhere he could come and think away from home. He liked to keep his business away from the apartment, particularly the side of his business that involved other operatives. Sammy was an old friend. They'd worked together in Iraq for a couple of years and shared some pretty intense moments, but he'd never even think of inviting him into his home.

"We need to think of it as just another job, Sammy. We don't even need to get the thing off the premises. All we need to do is ensure that it's executed publicly and on the record. We either need to find a way of doing it without detection or we need a patsy, someone who'll do the work for us if we set it up."

Sammy pondered, his meaty hands cupping the sides of his face. "You know, a lot of folk really worshipped those people. There's a lot of angry fans out there who don't like what's happened."

"And how do you know that?"

"Well it's Jenny, you know? She buys all them celebrity lifestyle magazines and those rags are full of it. Some of them fucking celebs are making a charity record to raise funds for dead movie stars or some shit. And on the internet, there's all sorts of shit being stirred up."

"Now here I was thinking they were making millions off the back of this in Vegas."

"Oh, sure they are. Hey, most folks will pay a fortune to get near Tom Cruise or Jennifer Aniston. The fact they're dead ain't gonna change a thing. You know they charge twenty dollars a time for you to get your photo taken with one of them?"

"I've said it before Sammy: it's one fucked-up world."

"But there's always gonna be the people who go hardcore on these things—protestors and shit. That's what we need, someone we can get in the room with the right weapon, make sure we ain't got our fingerprints anywhere near it. We'll just aim him and point him in the right direction."

"That simple?"

"Hey, security in the place is likely to be as tight as my sister's asshole—it's gonna take some planning. But yeah, Trav, this could be the easiest ten million anyone ever made."

Sammy had taken advantage of his wife's on-line proclivities and within forty eight hours, they found their man. Or woman, as it had turned out. Her name was *Louischick04* and she was as demented as anyone Travis had ever encountered.

"This broad is perfect. She's mad as a ditch full of turkeys, Trav. Jenny just had to ask the right questions, make the right suggestions to her, and she was like putty. She wants to get Louis Starr out of there so bad all we need to do is put a weapon in her hand and get her through the fucking door."

Travis had read through a copy of the chats Sammy's wife had had with their potential patsy. She seemed like the real deal. She had so much anger you could almost taste it in the erratic, clumsy typing and the vicious vocabulary. She wanted her idol as dead as Travis did, but not for profit—just out of misplaced love for a stranger she'd built her misguided fantasies around.

"I tell you again, Sammy, the internet is only good for cheap CDs and jerking off. This woman is a fucking psycho."

"She sure is Trav, and she'll make us so rich we'll never have to work again."

Travis hoped so. He dug around, called in a few favors, and got himself a schematic of the Hall of Living Celebrities, as their target's new home was named. It had been called 'Dead Celebrities' for all of an afternoon, until someone from the government had added their two cents. It was inside what had previously been Planet Hollywood, the casino having been eagerly torn out to make way for a much easier money spinner. There were upward of sixty zombies inside, and new ones were arriving all the time as staff at the internment centers suddenly realized that the snarling monstrosity in the corner was Tom Selleck or Meg Ryan. The zombies were held behind reinforced transparent plasti-glass—bullet-proof but vulnerable to certain explosives. There were metal detectors and full body searches at the entrance to the building and at the celebrity gallery. Anything Sammy tried to smuggle in would need to avoid both. This was where Travis and Sammy earned their rep.

"I've booked the nutjob a ticket to Vegas for next Monday and I've arranged that we'll aim to be in the hall at the same time—three fifteen exactly. We'll bring down the barrier in front of Louis Starr, she'll shoot him in the head, and make sure everyone sees her. She's got some little speech she wants to make, so we'll have time to make sure the guards are busy before she opens fire."

"Okay." Travis thought his plan was as good as they were likely to get without going for a frontal assault on the place, and the dangers of civilian casualties that would create. He didn't care that any passersby might be killed. Hell, he'd shoot a football team of five-year-olds for the promise of ten million cash, but once civilians were involved, the response tended to escalate as a consequence.

He rolled up the plans. "Let's get to Vegas."

Travis had never been to Vegas before, and it lived up to his low expectations. The city was a like a circus of poor taste, and he found the temptation to start kidney punching fat tourists almost overwhelming.

"Why the fuck would people choose to come to this shithole?"

"Hey, it ain't so bad, Trav. Find some hot piece of ass to follow you around, get coked up, then hit the blackjack tables. It's like being James fucking Bond for the weekend. And I tell you, the all-you-can-eat surf and turf buffets in this town are to die for."

"We live in different worlds, Sammy."

"You should come visit mine some time, Trav. It's a hell of a lot more fun here!"

They managed to get into Planet Hollywood without a fuss. Neither of them expected any different. Getting in was always the easy part—it was getting out that normally caused the problems. They passed through the detectors without a hitch, the pat down from the bored security guards being perfunctory. This pleased Travis. He could sense the complacency in the staff, and could tell that none of them genuinely expected any trouble. It might go easier than he'd thought.

"We're fifteen minutes early," Travis said.

"Cool. Let's go and look at the stiffs."

The Hall of Living Celebrities was packed with upward of a hundred tourists, all waddling from exhibit to exhibit *oohhing* and *ahhing* at the faces they'd only previously seen leering at them from their TV screens.

The celebrities' cages were recessed back from the thoroughfare that ran through the hall, thick red rope marking the boundary between their space and their guests. A red carpet ran the length of the hall, as if there was still something glamorous about the twisted scenario. There were queues forming in front of some of the cages as gawking pleasure seekers waited in line to have their photographs taken in the same frame as a decaying ghoul that used to be an idol.

"Oh what a wonderful world," Travis sighed.

Sammy, on the other hand, loved it all. "Would you look at that?" he said in gleeful awe. He wandered over to a plastic cell where a zombie clawed at the glass. It was dressed in a baseball jacket, but the jacket was smeared with dried blood and other fluids that its rapidly putrefying body leaked out. "Charlie *fucking* Sheen. Hell, you look cleaner than you've been in years, you son-of-a-bitch."

Travis couldn't look at the thing for too long. He just couldn't understand the fascination. He'd seen the zombies at far too close a quarter during the Event, and had seen the cold absence of humanity in their faces, the horrible truths they represented. It just seemed that everyone else wanted to turn them into a circus act. Travis wasn't sure he'd ever be able to do that.

They wandered along the hallway past actors and singers, some of them almost fresh, others so damaged it was difficult to reconcile the shambling corpse with the looped videos that ran behind them, showing them alive and in their showbiz element. Sammy got over-excited at the sight of Madonna, even though she was simply hunched in the corner, gnawing on a bone like a much-abused dog.

Three o'clock mercifully arrived. The two of them retreated, found separate cubicles and retrieved their respective ceramic gun parts from their uncomfortable hiding places. Travis assembled them, loading the pistol with three bullets—enough to do the job with something to spare, they figured. Then they made their way back to the hall.

Louischick04 had been told to wear a t-shirt adorned with the face of her idol and red-framed sunglasses. They needn't have bothered with those details, as it was obvious who she was the moment they looked for her. She was small and dumpy, the kind of face that even a parent would struggle to love. She was staring into the cage in which Louis Starr growled and dribbled in a manner not totally unlike his stage performances. His long, jet back hair had been pulled out in clumps and one half of his face was gouged and torn, but he looked better than some of the other residents. There were tears running down Louischick04's face as they approached her.

"You ready for this?" Travis asked her softly when he joined her.

She sniffed and wiped a hand across her nose, spreading snot over her face. "You bet I am," she said through her tears. He passed her the pistol, letting it slide from his sleeve into her hand.

"I'm going to shatter the glass. As soon as that happens you'll need to do it fast while there's still confusion. Then drop the gun and get the fuck out of here as quick as you can."

"I know what to do."

"Good." He shared a look with his partner. Sammy scanned the hall, took in the positions of the security guards and saw that the two cameras overseeing their position had moved away on their regular arc.

"Good to go," Sammy said.

Travis opened the cover of his watch, withdrew the compact explosive, and threw it without ceremony at the plasti-glass. It slapped onto the surface like bird shit onto a windshield.

Travis counted down from five to one, backing away from Louis Starr's cell. At zero, there was a muffled boom and the explosion went off, no louder than a firecracker but with enough force to punch a series of heavy cracks into the plastic. The explosion didn't make the zombie so much as twitch. It hammered on the glass again and this time it gave, falling in thick chunks to the ground.

There was pandemonium in the hall. This was what Travis had counted on. The moment the shock of the explosion passed and the crowd realized what was happening, they would panic and run for the exits. Security would be pressed back, and they wouldn't be able to get near to Louisechick04 in time to stop her.

She raised the pistol.

"Louis, you're like the coolest thing that ever happened to music. I love you! What these people have done to you is obscene!" She turned to look back at the retreating crowd. "This is for all the

Dead Celebrities! The Transient Liberation Front has spoken! We will not rest until freedom is granted to all of you!"

"I don't like the sound of that," Sammy panted as they pushed their way through the crowd.

Louisechick04 swung the pistol away from Louis and aimed it at a white box hanging high on the wall above them. She fired twice, and both bullets hit their target, the box igniting in a flare of broken circuitry. There was a fizzing sound and then all the cages on that side of the hall swung open, releasing their occupants.

"Sammy, I'm never going to ask your wife to get a patsy again," Travis said as he elbowed a fat Alabaman behind him, pushing her to the floor to give him a better chance of escape.

A klaxon began to sound over the screaming. Without warning, a sheer metal shutter slid down like a guillotine over the exit. The first of the fleeing civilians crashed into it, while the rest quickly followed and crushed the ones in front against the sudden barrier. From their position near the back of the fleeing crowd, Travis and Sammy could hear bones snapping with the force of the impact.

Louis Starr staggered awkwardly out of his cage. Louischick04 stood with her arms out to him in welcome. He didn't pass up the opportunity, and his teeth were on her face as soon as she was in biting distance.

When the crowd realized they couldn't get through the barrier of steel and crushed flesh, they turned and headed back into the hall, the freed zombies now joining their ranks as they lumbered from their cages. Travis discovered that his way was blocked. He had to tread back over the tourist he'd left sprawling and put one foot in her well-fed gut to propel him. He couldn't hear her scream over the others. He fixated on the pistol. Just one bullet left, but it might be enough.

Security guards fired their weapons somewhere behind him. The screams reached a new intensity, coupled now with the hungry sounds of the undead feast. Travis lost sight of Sammy, and didn't really care. In these situations, self-preservation was the key.

A zombie twisted its broken frame into his path. He thought he recognized her, a blonde-haired thing that snarled at him as he approached. She was some sort of socialite named after a European hotel. Travis didn't think about it too hard. Instinctively, he grabbed hold of a fire extinguisher, lifted it in front of his head like a battering ram, and smashed it into her. It went through her face, breaking bone and sinew as it went, and she fell to the floor in a legally dead heap.

"That's another family that owes me a percentage," he said as he climbed over her. Just a few feet in front of him, Louis Starr was still eating his number one fan, wolfing down a fistful of her entrails like a dog with a string of sausage. Travis sped up, increased his momentum, and kicked the corpse as hard as he could, sending it spinning onto the red carpet. Without pause, he put the extinguisher down and hunted across Louischick04's body, ignoring the blood and black stuff that flowed from deep within her. It was still there—the pistol was just beside her hand. Travis thanked whatever god happened to be looking over him that day and clutched the pistol in his grateful palm.

Louischick04 opened her eyes. A gurgling, blood-drowned hiss escaped from her throat. She was back already. Travis picked up the extinguisher and used both hands to thrust it down upon her head. It exploded under the impact like a watermelon filled with offal.

"You cost me ten million fucking dollars," Travis spat, and hammered the extinguisher down again, just for his own piece of mind. Louis Starr was getting back to his lifeless feet, snarling with hunger at the man who'd been paid to put him out of everyone's misery. Travis pointed the pistol at him.

One bullet left.

He looked behind him. Most of the crowd were now in a fight for their lives, battling back the dead with whatever tools they had to hand, which largely meant cameras and fanny packs. There was no sign of any organized security—they must have fallen with the rest. Under a pile of decaying but animated flesh, Travis could see Sammy, his face taut with agony, his body being torn and eaten. Sammy saw him, caught his eye, then gave him a perverse smile as he was eaten alive by dead superstars.

"I always wanted to dine with the stars, Trav!" he yelled through a mouthful of blood.

One bullet and no way out.

Travis put the gun to his temple as Louis Starr and half the cast of Friends descended on him.

"Showbiz sucks," he whispered before blowing his brains out.

"Finally tonight, some celebrity news! Despite the recent incident at the Hall of Living Celebrities, organizers say the show will go on due to public demand. Protestors have been lobbying to have the exhibit closed after the death or transience of thirty visitors last week following an act of sabotage by a member of a group calling itself the Transient Liberation Front.

"However, ticket sales for the show have risen dramatically since the announcement that Johnny Depp will be unveiled as the new star attraction this weekend. Organizers have assured us that new safety measures have been undertaken and no repeat of last week's atrocity will occur.

"The interim government has refused to comment on the issue, amidst suggestions that the public may soon get the opportunity to see transient figures from government and politics on display as well. This follows reports earlier in the week suggesting that the discovery of a hidden bunker belonging to the Bush family has unearthed a number of very high profile transients.

"Whatever happens, this is certainly an exciting time to be a celebrity spotter! We'll be back tomorrow night! In the meantime, keep watching the stars!"

MORNING AT GRAVESIDE

ASH HARTWELL

The first rays of the early morning sun were just beginning to appear on the eastern horizon when Billy tip-toed past his mother's room. Taking care not to stand on a loose floorboard, he crept down the stairs. He paused by the front door, listening for signs of movement from the floor above.

Satisfied that he had not disturbed his mother's sleep, he stepped into the cold morning air. Pulling the hood of his coat up, the young man walked down the path and across the road before turning to walk directly towards the sun. Billy walked calmly with his head down. There was no need to draw attention to himself. In his experience that only led to trouble.

There was nobody about as he reached the junction and turned right, towards the open parkland. He cut through a large hole in the bushes, and without looking up, walked towards the small metal gate that marked the alleyway on the other side of the park.

Billy had made this walk countless times over the last few months and had no need to look up to see where he was going. After a few minutes, he walked through the gate leading into the alleyway that cut through between the houses overlooking the cemetery. The early morning sun had not yet breached the alleyway which was still shrouded in darkness. Billy stopped for a moment to peer into the mouth of the alley.

It appeared to be empty. But then again, he'd thought the boy's bathroom at school was empty of people and then *BAM!*, he'd found himself upside down in a flushing toilet, thanks to the school bullies.

Billy took a couple of faltering steps into the darkness, then waited.

No one came running out of the shadows intent on sticking his head into a flushing vortex. He continued his journey, his steps gaining confidence with each stride. He lifted his head up and strode purposefully out of the far end of the alley. Just the way Grandpa had told him when he'd walked behind his father's coffin.

"Hold your head up high. Show them your face. Show them your pride." Billy still remembered his grandfather's words like it was yesterday. The last seven years had flown by, taking Grandpa with them. It appeared that cancer was a tougher opponent than the Vietcong.

He waited while a solitary car rolled down the road, then crossed over to the wrought-iron gates of the cemetery. He pushed one open enough for him to slide through, then walked up the long gravel path. After a few minutes of walking between weeping angels, elaborate crosses and marble tombstones, Billy stopped by a simple white stone cross that marked the plot of earth that had been Grandpa's home for the last four months.

Standing in silence, he read the familiar words carved in the stone. Once he finished, he repeated the last line, this time in a loud voice that carried on the early morning air. "Semper Fi."

He sat down on the damp grass in front of his grandpa's headstone. "Hi there, Gramps. Mom and I miss you." He wiped a tear from his eye.

He was silent for a few minutes, just enjoying the sun as it began to warm his back. Then he said, "Gramps I need to talk to you. I need to know what to do." He began to pick his thumbnail, a sure fire way of telling he was nervous. It was a trait he had picked up as a child and never grown out off.

"There are these boys at school. The usual punk-ass kids that think they own the place. They sell drugs around the schools campus and steal students and school property. Anyone who gets in their way gets threatened…or worse." Billy started to bite his thumbnail. He was unsure why he was telling all this to a sculptured slab of stone but he had to tell someone.

"Yesterday, I saw them handing something to Joey. You remember Joey, he lives next door. Anyway they saw me watching them and later they stuffed my head down the toilet…" He fell silent, ashamed of what had happened.

After a few minutes, he stood up. "Well I'd better get going, Gramps. Don't know what I expected you to do." He was just about to turn away when he noticed a patch of grass in the center of his grandfather's grave bulge upwards then split open. He stared down at the small slit of exposed soil, trying to comprehend what he was seeing.

In the middle of the slit there were what appeared to be two fingers protruding from the damp earth. Billy bent forward to get a better look just as the fingers disappeared back into the dark hole. He tentatively took half a step forward, then stopped in his tracks as a large fist punched through the top soil. The grass around the flailing arm now reached upwards from the earth, fingers stretched towards the sky, then began to fall back in on itself.

Billy scampered backwards. Part of him wanted to turn around and run. The dirt heaved upwards as a head and shoulders appeared above the ground. The body arched back and forth, desperate to free itself from the sucking effect of the damp soil that tried to pull it back, as if the Devil himself were intent on preventing its escape.

With slow determined movements, the decomposing figure pulled itself across the grass. Its large hands clawed the well-manicured lawn, its feet kicking free of the hole from which it has ascended.

Billy had to take a few steps back as the pungent and overpowering stench of decay assailed his nostrils and burned his throat. He gagged, fighting the urge to vomit on the surrounding graves.

The previously dead and buried body lay face down on the early morning grass, as if enjoying some long forgotten pleasure. Then, with a gentle rustling from the loose clothing hanging limply from the emaciated frame, the dead man began to stand.

Steadily, the figure rose to its feet and for the first time in months Billy looked into the face of his grandfather.

Sure the face was thinner than it had been when he was alive and Grandpa never used to walk around with his eyes stitched closed. Then again, Grandpa used to have eyeballs.

Billy's cadaverous Grandpa tugged on his disheveled Marine Corps uniform to straighten it and began a shuffling march across the cemetery, heading in the general direction of the main gate. Even with the advantage of being alive, Billy struggled to keep pace with his grandfather's determined strides. Once at the gate, the undead soldier slipped through the opening, and turning smartly on his heel, he set off down the road.

Occasionally, someone would pass them by, but no one took any notice of the young man walking proudly with his sick-looking Grandpa. Billy ensured that they stopped at the pedestrian crossing by pulling back on his grandfather's hand. When the little green man appeared on the lighted sign, Billy gave him a gentle nudge in the back to start him moving again.

The two of then turned into the school gates just before the bell sounded. Several girls were sitting on the steps that surrounded the flag pole, from which fluttered the Stars and Stripes. They looked up at the curious old man who stood in front of them, then as realization spread across their faces, they screamed and scattered in all directions.

Billy's Grandpa watched them run away with empty eyes, a half-smile appearing to cross his face, before he continued on into the school's busy corridor.

Students ran in all directions as Billy's grandfather strode down the main corridor. Occasionally, he pushed someone out of his path.

One young footballer tried to stand in their way, encouraged by his desire to be brave in front of his girlfriend. Billy's un-dead guardian picked the high school line backer up by the throat and threw him through the frosted glass panel of a classroom door.

A few minutes later, the corridor was deserted and Billy and his grandfather were standing outside the boys' bathroom. The sound of laughter could be heard coming from inside.

The walking dead warrior turned towards Billy and saluted before charging through the door.

At first Billy heard the abuse shouted at his grandfather: "Hey, old man. I think you got lost. The old folks' home is down the road…" After that there was a choked scream followed by the sound of people yelling. Another scream that caused Billy to shudder was followed by a moment of unnatural quiet that seemed to last an eternity.

The silence was broken by a young man appearing in the bathroom doorway. He opened his mouth to shout but never uttered a sound. A large hand appeared on either side of his head, and with a slight twist, pulled the head clear off the boy's shoulders.

Billy watched as the hands pulled the severed head back through the doors and out of sight.

The body remained standing, as if unsure as to what it should do, then with a gentle sigh it sank to the floor, blood spurting from the gaping neck hole the entire time.

After a few minutes of silence, Billy calmly walked into the bathroom. The walls were covered in blood. Some of it was finely sprayed on and formed gentle arcs, while some was roughly smeared over a larger area.

Billy could taste the metallic scent in the air. In the corner, his grandfather was feasting on the prone body of one of his victims.

Billy walked over to the stalls. They were all empty, the doors wide open. Three of the toilets contained severed heads.

With a smile, Billy pushed each flush button before turning and walking out.

SAVE THE CHILDREN

GABINO INGLESIAS

"You better be right about this, Parker!" Sergeant Malone's voice was barely audible over the sound of the roaring wind that whipped through the SUV's open windows.

Brian Parker nodded at the screaming cop while his right hand flew to the top of his head and tried to hold his helmet in place. He wished someone would have helped him figure out how to fasten the thing onto his noggin before they pushed him into the vehicle.

The coil lock wire binding of Parker's reporter's notebook, which he'd instinctively stuck in his back pocket before leaving the house, was digging deep into his right buttock with every movement the vehicle made.

The fingers on the reporter's left hand were wrapped so tightly around the handle next to his head that his knuckles turned white. Parker's bicep ached from the strain, and pain shot throughout his body from the rough ride along the unpaved road. Although the situation was bad, he wasn't about to complain. Every nerd and pencil pusher joke in the book had been thrown his way in the preceding hours.

Sergeant Malone said something unintelligible to the driver. Based on the huge vein that seemed about ready to pop out of Malone's neck, and the spittle that had flown out of his mouth, Parker guessed the man was screaming again. Abrasive seemed to be the only mood the sergeant was capable of displaying. He was a testosterone Molotov cocktail.

The crunch of dirt and gravel under the tires and the howl of the wind was all Parker heard for a while. Finally, the police vehicle skidded to a halt and bodies jumped out of the vehicle as if propelled by tightly coiled springs.

A dilapidated, three-story building stood in front of them with gaping, broken windows and a dark mat of English ivy running up its walls. By itself, the edifice would have been considered creepy. For Parker, who had an inkling of the nightmares they would surely encounter within its walls, the abandoned building was like a looming monster that hoped to lure them in.

Once all the bodies had spilled out of the vehicles and everyone had assembled in front of Sgt. Malone, orders were screamed. In a few seconds, everyone was darting around with an obvious sense of purpose. Parker was left standing next to the squad car, holding his camera bag in one hand and his reporter's notebook in the other. The pain in his backside was slowly ebbing away and becoming a weird, pulsating itch. Despite the physical discomfort, it was really the sense of aimlessness that was gnawing at the reporter.

Sgt. Malone cut his mental meandering in half with another scream. "Parker! Put that damn camera away, get your ass behind me, and keep your eyes open!"

Parker felt like a child. He'd expected to be handed a weapon at some point, but it had never happened. To go into the building with the team and have no way of defending himself struck him as preposterous. Fear gripped his testicles with an icy hand and squeezed.

Finding the place where the Haitians had been taking the kids had given Parker a sense of elation that he'd never felt before while doing his job. Convincing the police, and his editor, that he had sufficient evidence to bust the place and end the madness made Parker feel like he was on the brink of becoming a hero. The night raid played out in his mind as something beautiful and reckless, like a scene out of a Clint Eastwood movie. He desired an adrenaline rush and the sense that justice had been done because of his initiative. Now, standing next to the squad car with the sergeant yelling at him and no gun, he felt lost and emasculated.

A tall, jacked cop stuffed in an undersized shirt approached the sergeant at a trot.

"The team is ready to go, sir," the man growled while Parker stared at the massive veins snaking down the man's cartoonish arms. The cop's voice made him think of a snarling beast. The image of an overdeveloped ape on steroids came to mind. Sgt. Malone nodded and turned to pierce Parker with his eyes once again. "If half of what you told us is actually going down in there, you better stay on your toes, Parker. You ready to go?"

The tight, cold clutch that fear had on his testicles made Parker nod instead of utter a response. Having his voice break in this testosterone fest would be the equivalent of getting caught stroking his meat to gay porn by a pack of ravenous skinheads.

"Just stay behind me like a shadow and duck if any shots come our way. You got that? The last thing I need right now is a dead journalist on my hands."

Parker nodded again and couldn't help feeling like a bobble-head doll in a bulletproof vest. Parker and Malone joined the team at the entrance to the ominous-looking building just as four massive cops dressed all in black and wearing body armor and helmets smashed the door with a battering ram. The sound of the ram hitting the door was enough to make Parker think about heading back to the SUV. But with his manhood on the line and the story of a lifetime on the other side of the door, he stood his ground and pushed the desire to flee out of his skull.

The door exploded inward on the second hit, flying off its hinges and crashing to the floor with a loud boom that echoed inside the building and reminded Parker of a gunshot.

A dozen bodies crossed the threshold before the sergeant ventured in. Parker stayed so close to the man that he feared bumping into his back and sending Malone into a screaming rage.

Once inside, the team split up and only the bob of flashlights attached to rifles and helmets was visible down the huge corridor that opened up to the right of the entrance. Parker watched as the team spread out into smaller groups and their lights disappeared through different, cavernous doorways. The sound of doors being kicked in bounced off the walls and confused the hell out of Parker.

The gloom inside the building was a special kind of darkness that Parker had never seen before. Rather than a lack of light, the air inside the building seemed to be tainted by a thick, murky smoke. The pungent smell of rotted wood, mold, and decay invaded his nostrils and made the darkness seem even more menacing.

Roughly thirty seconds after the team crossed the threshold, the first shot rang out. A gurgled scream followed. The sound died quickly. A frigid icicle ran up Parker's back, playing his vertebrae like a xylophone and coming to rest at the base of his neck. He looked down at his watch and scribbled the time in his notebook. A chronicle of the bust would get him major recognition: times, names and places needed to be painfully accurate.

Just as Parker scribbled down 11:37 p.m. on his notebook, the entire place erupted in a confusing maelstrom of gunfire and screams. Keeping track of the dead would be a hard task.

A large figured stumbled out of one of the rooms and ambled its way toward Parker and Malone. The sergeant raised his weapon and fired twice. In the beam of light coming from Malone's helmet, Parker could see the approaching figure and the two dark, ragged holes that exploded over its chest. The hulking figure was completely naked and its distended belly and lumbering gait suggest three hundred pounds of flesh. Its gray skin sagged as if a skinnier man was hiding under all that blubber.

Malone stared, frozen in his firing stance. Parker could read the sergeant's thoughts like an open book: the man had taken two bullets to the chest and was still coming at them.

Suddenly, a shot rang out and the left side of the fat man's head was pulverized, sending an eyeball streaking through the air. The eye landed about six inches from them. Malone stepped on it. A loud pop was followed by a squishy sound that Parker knew would forever remain engraved in his brain.

The team started moving again and Parker kept his eyes glued to the back of Malone's neck. As they reached the fat man, Parker once more became a victim of his own curiosity and peeked at the body.

The fat man's arms and legs were scarred with cuts that oozed puss, and in the space where his genitals were supposed to be, tattered, decaying flesh hung in strips. Parker looked away and concentrated on walking and breathing.

The sergeant moved slowly as he checked the first room on the right. Despite the fact that the room had already been checked, Malone seemed on edge. In the second room they entered, sprawled feet immediately came within the confines of Parker's peripheral vision. Malone pointed his flashlight toward the feet that were next to the door and then looked at the entire room. Parker couldn't help but take a peek.

Two bodies.

The first was a skinny black man with some kind of skin disease. Parker forced himself to look at the man and take mental notes.

No shirt.

No shoes.

Dirty, torn jeans.

A pool of blood was slowly spreading underneath the man. The liquid came from two dark holes visible on his body: one over his heart and one on the right side of his abdomen.

About five feet away, another shirtless man in tattered shorts was lying on the floor. His limbs twitching oddly, he struggled to get up, despite the fact that the left side of his torso had been blown away and his arm and part of his shoulder were near the opposite wall of the room. His ashen flesh was full of lesions.

A muffled snarl erupted from his mouth, along with a dark black syrup that had to be blood. The cop that was a mound of muscles that had spoken to Malone outside the house stood six feet away from the body, pressed against a wall. His shaking rifle was trained on the twitching man.

Sgt. Malone walked over to the body and Parker slowly moved behind him. The sergeant peeled his eyes away from the convulsing figure on the floor and looked up at the muscled cop as he approached.

"What the hell are you waiting for, Cortez?" Malone barked.

"I...nothing, sir."

A sound came from behind them. Malone and Parker spun around. The black man on the floor was getting up. His right arm hung limply by his side as if it were boneless.

Cortez fired twice into the man's chest, forcing him to take a step back. Instead of falling down, the black man snarled and a mysterious, gooey clump slithered out of his mouth and fell to the floor with a plop. Parker felt a scream rise in his throat.

Cortez beat the reporter to the punch, immediately silencing his own scream under a hail of bullets from his rifle that rapidly crawled up the man's chest to his face. The entire left side of the man's face was destroyed, and gore splattered on the wall behind him while chunks of flesh and skull flew out the door.

Malone turned back to the twitching man on the floor in front of them. Cortez's eyes looked about to pop out of his skull as they remained on the slumped black man on the floor like trained dogs.

"Fuck!" The single word came out of Malone's mouth a fraction of a second before a bullet from his SIG 556 obliterated the top of the skull of the man on the floor. The brainless body went limp and dark slime began to ooze out of what was left of the head. An ache in Parker's chest announced to him that he'd been holding his breath.

Malone started to advance toward the body and details began to appear under the approaching light. A thick, vile-smelling mixture of brackish fluid and what looked like intestines slowly seeped out of the huge cavity on the corpse's left side.

Bile slid into Parker's esophagus, and its acidic burn gurgled in his throat. He swallowed hard, looked away, and concentrated on breathing through his mouth.

"Get your ass behind me, Parker!"

He hurried to catch up with the sergeant. He hadn't even noticed that his feet weren't moving when Malone approached the dead man.

More shots echoed down the hallway.

"What the hell was this place, anyway?" Malone asked.

"It...it was a school," Parker replied.

"A school? You sure about that?"

"Yes. It was called the Travis State School. They worked with mentally challenged boys that..."

"You have to come see this, Sergeant," interrupted a voice from the door. A hulking figure stood on the threshold, a silhouette outlined by dark gray. The man nervously shifted his weight from one foot to the other.

Parker and Malone followed him down a dark hall with Cortez bringing up the rear. They turned left at the end of the hallway and entered a massive room. The decrepit, crumbling wooden tables and tall, wrecked ceiling told Parker the place had once been a plant nursery. In the middle of the room, the long tables had been pushed to the sides and a big cage sat in the cleared area.

The cage contained lumbering, skulking children.

The nervous zigzagging of the flashlight beams allowed Parker to catch only glimpses of the moving bodies. The children looked gray and malnourished. Their hair was matted to their heads and their clothes were full of gore. Some of them appeared to have serious injuries and were covered in blood. They were walking around aimlessly without acknowledging the people surrounding them. Parker was as curious as he was repelled and appalled. Being sure of what the Haitians were doing to the kids and seeing it with his own eyes were two very different things.

The cops were quiet, the pungent smell of putrid meat permeating the room.

Malone was the first to approach the cage. His face's contortion of disgust was obvious despite the room's thick darkness.

"What the fuck did they do to these kids?" The question was spat rather than asked.

"We have no idea, sir, but they haven't said a word since we came in here," a young cop said. His hands shook so badly that his rifle rattled. Parker noticed everyone in the room was at least ten feet from the cage and visibly on edge. He wished he had a flashlight, too. And a gun.

"I told you they were turning them into zombies," Parker mumbled.

Every pair of eyes in the room turned to Parker. An invisible, cold hand like the one that was clutching his balls since they'd arrived suddenly started doing the same to his throat.

"What the hell are you talking about, Parker? Zombies? As in the flesh-eating undead things in God-awful movies?" Malone asked with what seemed like an accusatory tone in his voice.

"Not like in the movies, Sergeant, like in Haiti. The Haitians have practiced zombification for centuries. They mix together certain chemicals and..."

"For Christ's sake, Parker, spare me the mumbo-jumbo explanation and tell me what you know!" Malone barked angrily.

"Just what I told you two days ago. After Haiti was devastated by the earthquake a year and a half ago, some Haitian drug lords came to the states and set up shop here. Children started disappearing a few months ago in or near Zilker Park, and I decided..."

The sound of a fast-moving body hitting the wall of the cage made every man in the room jump back and raise their weapons. A boy of about ten, with his black eyes set on Malone, scratched at the cage. All flashlights were targeted on the boy. The beams of light shook violently. The boy's snarling mouth was full of dark stumps where teeth once were and his faced looked like it had taken a beating and then spent a week at the bottom of a dumpster.

"Somebody get some real lights in here!" Malone shouted. "Cortez, Albrecht! Get behind me and keep your weapons ready."

The three men formed a small V formation and Malone unhurriedly walked the twelve feet that stood between him and the growling child. The boy in the cage became more aggressive with every step forward Malone took. With so many flashlights on the dead child, Parker could clearly see the grayish, splotchy skin. He was hardly a doctor, but an advanced degree of putrefaction was obvious even to the untrained eye.

A piece of the boy's lower lip dangled from the right corner of his snarling mouth. The piece was big enough to be noticed even under the dark sludge dripping from his mouth. A small indentation under the boy's right eye reminded Parker of overripe fruit that had been thumbed too hard. The blue shorts and black t-shirt covering his small body were almost completely covered with a dark liquid that continuously dribbled out of his stump-filled mouth.

Then Parker shifted his focus and took in another boy that was coming toward them behind the first one. He decided that the gloom, and everything that he'd witnessed, were playing tricks on his mind. What his eyes were registering was not possible.

The second boy reached the fence and started snarling just like the first one. His face was much better than the first kid, but he was shirtless, and there was a gaping hole yawning open right below his sternum. As the boy moved and the light changed angles on him, Parker could see glimpses of white at the back of the hole. He realized he was looking at the child's spinal cord through the empty space where his bowels were supposed to be. Vomit erupted from Parker's throat before he even realized it was happening.

A racket by the door startled everyone in the room as two men rushed in, carrying a couple of construction lights on stands and a long cable. The lights were set up in seconds, and the room was suddenly inundated with white, blinding light. Parker could almost feel the quick contraction of his pupils. It took him a few seconds before his eyes could focus again.

The brighter light had apparently announced their presence to the other ambling bodies in the cage. Every child sprung to life violently, frantically pawing at the fence and snarling savagely. Parker was suddenly overloaded with gory details. A tall, thin boy of about six or seven was coming at the cage with no arms. To his right, a small girl in a dress that had once been blue was holding on to a gore-covered teddy bear and baring her teeth his way. Her eye sockets were empty. Another girl limped toward the group with a foot that twisted all the way out every time she took a step.

Parker looked at Malone. The sergeant was the only one who hadn't taken a few steps back. In fact, he continued to approach the cage even after they had flooded the room with light. He was about eight inches away from the first boy, his face contorted into an intense, seemingly painful frown.

"Holy Mother of God! Are you sure these are the missing kids, Parker?" Malone asked.

"I'm positive," Parker croaked. The strength of his voice was shattered by fear, but none of the men in the room seemed to notice.

A week ago, he'd followed two Haitians almost all the way back to this same building before fear had sent him running back to the office. He'd presented his editor and the Chief of Police with the blurry pictures of the two Haitians pushing a crying child into the back of a car at Zilker Park. Now, he began to feel guilty for not stopping them sooner.

"Do you think a doctor could...fix them?" Malone asked.

"No," Parker replied. "They're...I think they're dead."

"Dead? Did you just say that you think they're dead? This little guy here seems pretty animated to me. In fact, he looks downright willing to...do something to me if I open that door. How can you say they're dead?" The sergeant's face was contorting further.

"They were brought back to life as zombies," Parker said with an exhausted tone. "How many times do I have to explain it to you?"

Malone bared his teeth and replied almost without moving his lips. "You'll explain it to me as many fucking times as I deem necessary. You got that?"

Once more, Parker's response was reduced to an almost imperceptible nod.

"All right, listen up!" Malone yelled, addressing the men around him. "We need to make sure these kids don't do whatever it is they seem to be aching to do."

"What exactly are you planning?" Parker asked.

"That guy back there stopped twitching the second his head was gone, so I'm gonna use that same method a few more times," the sergeant said.

"You can't just...kill them all!" Parker shouted.

With four powerful strides, Malone was within two inches of Parker's face.

"I can do as I damn well please, Mr. Reporter," he hissed in Parker's cringing face. "You said these kids are already dead, so what fucking difference does it make? You want me to bring that boy back to his mother looking like a deranged, mangy beast? How about that one there with no damn intestines? You think we should drop him off at Granny's house for dinner? I have no idea what's going on here, but those things in there aren't children anymore."

A sudden flare of courage warmed Parker's gut and he uncoiled himself a bit from his scared crouch. "I won't let you slaughter these kids," he said before realizing the words were out of his mouth. "I need to do some more research, maybe there's still something we can do for them if..."

Malone turned away from him. "Johnson! Please remove Parker from the premises immediately."

A second later, a monstrously large hand seized Parker by the shoulder. He turned to see the vascular gorilla that had spoken to Malone before now had a grin on his face. Violence and strength radiated from the enormous man. Parker looked back at Malone but he couldn't bring himself to speak up. The cage was rattling and the men around it looked more than eager to pull their triggers. Another yank provoked Parker to start walking. Inertia was driving him forward, his eyes remaining on the decomposing monstrosities in the cage. He said nothing as he was escorted down the hall by the vicious linebacker named Johnson.

Just as they were exiting the building, a cacophony of gunshots erupted behind them. It was still going on when the uniformed ape pushed Parker into the back of the SUV and slammed the door closed.

Parker withdrew a pen, and in his shaking fist, wondered what words could be used to describe the massacre of something that was already dead.

HERO'S END

VINCENZO BILOF

It was common knowledge that Springfield was a shithole, but for Cassius, it was the perfect mission.

The life of a thief suited him. He'd never enjoyed taking orders, even when companies were willing to pay him rations and ammunition to work on salvage teams out in the wasteland. But while sitting in the cabin of a Huey helicopter, Cassius couldn't help but think about the seemingly impossible task ahead of him.

He was supplied with the finest gear, the latest tech out of New York. Cassius figured he was on borrowed time—nobody would hire him. His reputation as a 'live at all costs' loner complimented the fact that his way proved he was right, but the job market dried up. Companies believed that men were needlessly wasted, so anyone who worked on his team would ask for an advance against the probability that they wouldn't survive. It was a 'murder loan.' The mercenaries borrowed the money because they were almost certainly not coming back alive, and the companies couldn't justify paying out so much money.

So, Cassius had enemies. But that didn't really matter. It didn't matter if he came back from his last job. Some would have said that the stoic man had a death wish. Some would have been right.

The routine drop out of the chopper reminded him of the beginning, in New York. While the walking dead terrorized the bustling metropolis, Cassius and his men were ordered to put out fires and watch everyone die. He was one of the few surviving veterans who'd served during the initial meltdown, and since those days, no other company ever came close to being able to trade for or find someone to pilot a helicopter. The New Yorkers ruled the skies.

But there were apparently exceptions.

There was a part of him that didn't want to admit that the mission contained a personal element: a long time ago, his sister had been in command of the first team to touch down in Springfield. She never came back.

When he was a teenager, he'd aspired to follow in his sister's footsteps. Nina was a war hero, having served two tours in Afghanistan. He'd joined the army not for love of his country, but to make his family as proud of him as they were of Nina.

They'd both been caught in the maelstrom of violence and confusion that brought their world down upon their heads. Neither one of them knew anything else than the life of a soldier, and the New York project had kept them involved. He'd never had an opportunity to serve and fight beside her, as was always his dream.

Springfield had always been his final destination. While he no longer understood the concept of fear, he often wrestled with the nagging dread that dictated that he, too, go to Springfield to hunt down the mythical object that many others had died for.

He was supposed to find and steal a legendary object that was simply called 'the helmet.'

Cassius landed in the middle of a concrete jungle. Twisted, rusted machinery mired in dust and disuse provided the narrow hills and valleys, while windowless municipal buildings loomed like staring skeletons. Dusty glass crunched beneath the mercenary's black combat boots. Broken television sets, cell phones, batteries, children's toys, clothes... collected when the looting began, they'd been left behind in the piles of garbage and debris. As the helicopter disappeared into the wall of clouds which shaded the ruins from the sun's light, Cassius checked his gear.

Clad in the gray camouflage fatigues that were becoming increasingly more difficult to come by, his weapons included a baseball bat that was sheathed behind his back, two handguns resting in holsters at each hip, and a submachine gun slung over his shoulder. A small complement of knives hung in the belt around his waist, along with the precious ammunition.

No food or water. He was on his own. He liked it that way.

He waited for a long moment as the helicopter drifted away. Its arrival would have roused both the living and the dead within the ruins from whatever reverie they'd lost themselves in. He expected to draw the dead out into the open. He'd been able to use the dead as a sort of shield against intervention from the living, and if he knew where they all were at once, it would make maneuvering through the ruins that much easier for him.

His last mission. He almost couldn't believe it. To celebrate, he removed a cigar from one of his pockets and lit it up, taking long, fiery drags while he waited in the silence.

Cassius placed the mask, which was in the likeness of a human skull, over his face and peered through the electronic screen over the eyes. The infrared would only show him the glaring presence of living creatures, most of them rats, possums, and other scavengers. He patiently waited in the middle of the broken avenue for someone to take a shot at him, at least. His possessions represented a treasure trove to anyone willing to make a move.

Amongst the wilderness of odd creatures that climbed over the ashen husks of hollow cars, Cassius spotted a human-shaped red glow. If it was alive, why didn't it move or try to attack the well-armed soldier? Cassius always enjoyed baiting his enemies.

It made everything a lot easier.

Cassius removed the mask and let it drop on a chain below his chin. Assuming the man already spotted him, the mercenary simply strode over and stood over him.

"Baseball bat," a voice quietly said from underneath a pile of rags.

Cassius nodded, "You've never seen one?"

"That's all you have for trade."

Cassius puffed on the cigar for a moment while the sun momentarily peeked from behind a rushing mass of cloud, and was again blocked. "Who said I wanted to trade?"

"You were standing there like you needed something. People only come to Springfield for one thing. And you're not exactly dressed like a tourist. If you are, then you should know that the burgers here suck."

"How many others come through here?"

"Now you want information? You don't offer anything for trade?"

Cassius couldn't help but smirk. The survivor thought himself clever. "The baseball bat."

A slow smile creased the lines of the vagrant's mouth. His face was black with grime and strands of his wild hair were streaked with gray. "Anyone ever tell you that you look like a young Kevin Bacon? The actor?"

"Don't waste my time," Cassius said with the cigar smoldering between his teeth.

"You're going to kill me after you get what you want. I know how this works. You'll give me the bat and I'll take you part of the way, and I'll slip away before you can waste me. It's a game. In this game, the mercenary thinks that he's in charge, that he holds the upper hand. The soldier thinks that he's the only one who's dangerous."

The man was a hard-ass. With his wordplay, he managed to secure himself a shred of respect. It would be easy just to take care of him and find someone else more willing to help.

As Cassius withdrew the cigar and tapped the ash at his feet, he inhaled deeply. The living dead were dragging their filthy, rotting bodies through the ruins. It was the smell he'd been waiting for.

"Let me draw my gun," the man suggested.

Cassius had to laugh. "You're a funny man. At least you asked."

"You're undecided about me, or else you would have done it already. Let me show you why I used you for bait."

The mercenary found himself semi-interested in the man's bravery. He was in a good mood, after all. It *was* his last mission. He'd never made decisions that were, in his estimation, 'dramatic,' he always killed when he needed to. That ability alone had made it impossible for him to live as a domesticated citizen. He was a wild animal, and he belonged in the wild.

"Let's see what you're packing."

"Name's Lenin," the man said, removing a massive, pearl-handled revolver. In two, steady hands, he pointed the gun down the road.

"I didn't ask," Cassius said and leaned against a hulk of indistinguishable metal. He folded his arms across his chest and continued to smoke the cigar. The slow, heavy silence of a windless, hot day in August made the sky seem larger, as if the world were a splendorous power that was rather clothed in the sun and the stars. The universe revolved around Earth.

"Unfriendlies sometimes carry loot with them," Lenin said.

Cassius was already impressed. The man clearly understood the New Yorker terminology for the walking corpses, and also understood that the creatures preferred to travel in groups. Lenin was an experienced survivor.

Four figures suddenly flooded into the street, clambering over the broken metal of a bygone populace. They jerked their limbs and ripped strips of their remaining flesh as they passed through the shattered remnants of nameless storefronts. Graffiti that had been rendered ancient by the wind's erosive powers was still visible upon the charred brick as the creatures oozed onto the street. One of them tripped along the edge of a pot-hole and collapsed forward onto the pavement. The other three dragged broken, twitching limbs, scraping their feet through shards of glass.

They were hunched, mangled creatures with writhing worms dropping from their colorless, ruined threads. Flies flitted above the thin, wispy strands of hair which framed the shrunken faces and blood-filled eyes.

Lenin fired three precise shots from the gun, and all three corpses dropped. He casually approached the crawling fourth and blew a hole in the back of its head.

He turned around to Cassius. "What do you think?" he asked. The gun smoked in his fist. "I've trained myself how to shoot. Practiced with a slingshot. Never liked guns, though."

"You were a little slow," Cassius unfurled himself from the wall.

Lenin was already rummaging among the dead.

"Waste of ammo," Cassius said. "I'm moving on. You're going to lead the way for a while."

Lenin was already done. Whatever he'd discovered was small enough to be clasped tightly in his fist. "I know," he said. "I was showing off."

Cassius dropped the cigar to the pavement. There was no more time to enjoy life's little pleasures.

"They're all over Springfield," Lenin said, looking over his shoulder while gathering up his belongings, which included a back pack, a collection of knives, and the large revolver. "But you have limited intel on this place, don't you? They always just drop you people in and hope for the best."

Companies that usually expected high mortality rates didn't offer much in the way of information. Although it was counter-productive, there'd be a lot to gain for a lot of soldiers by taking out an entire team and making off with all of the loot. When the prizes were large, companies were usually prepared to send in one or two long-term employees who would clean up the mess and grab the desired salvage.

Cassius wasn't the first to try Springfield—this news wasn't a surprise to him. The fact that Lenin was well-versed in mercenary practices and had his own methods made Cassius nearly reconsider that it might be easier to just kill Lenin where he stood.

Lenin also recognized that Cassius knew almost nothing about the town or the origins behind its dangerous reputation.

The stranger moved quickly through the rubble, climbing deftly over broken girders while Cassius followed. A wall of clouds shaded the slow-moving plants and weeds that jutted from between the ruins as Mother Nature reclaimed its domain. Cassius slid the mask over his face once again and watched the tittering creatures scatter. Birds took flight overhead, and the empty silence was broken as clattering steel and twisting rubble were jostled.

The ruins seemed to transform into a steel mill in which the workers were invisible. Cassius and Lenin climbed over shattered walls and the blackened shells of abandoned cars. They seemed to be walking on top of the city.

When the soldier pulled the mask away from his face, he wasn't surprised to see so many of the unbalanced, lazy figures swaying within the remnants of blasted buildings.

"They drop you guys in," Lenin said while the community of corpses awoke, "and I hang out near the spot. Usually your people want help, and some don't."

"You're still alive." Cassius nodded his head, impressed.

"Thanks for noticing," Lenin said. "It keeps life interesting, you know? I usually have something to do when mercs show up. Springfield has been very good to me."

Cassius unsheathed the baseball bat. A creature's emaciated skull poked through a car that rested on its side.

Cassius wound up and smacked the creature's face with the bat, following through with such force that the creature's head twisted completely around. With very little muscle and flesh left to support the corpse's bones, it was susceptible to easy breaks.

Lenin held a machete in his fist. The weapon was almost useless unless it was somehow sharp enough to cleave through bone, and even then, its wielder needed time and room to cleave a creature's head from its rotted body.

"You're a little older than the others," Lenin said without gasping. The man was in excellent physical condition, an advantage in the wasteland.

"Where're you taking me?" Cassius was frustrated. He'd somehow been duped into placing his trust in the stranger, and he seemed no closer to his goal.

A stretching, flesh-flaking claw caught the soldier by the pant leg. He stomped on the hand and turned to deliver a heavy swing to a creature that stood just behind him.

Lenin shoved a creature from atop a rubble pile. "If you want to steal the greatest treasure this side of New York, then you'll have to follow me. You won't find it on your own."

"Bullshit," Cassius sheathed the bat and the grip on his machine gun. "Where is everybody? This is supposed to be a thriving community."

"You've heard some of the rumors," Lenin stopped and wiped his forehead with a piece of the robe. "But this place is dead, and getting deader by the day."

"Where are they coming from?"

"They used to bring entire teams in here. This place has thrived because there was so much loot from the corpses. It was a trade town for a little while."

"And you've made a good living for yourself."

Lenin shrugged. "I've been here a while. I used to just lead guys like you straight into a trap, and I'd get a share of the action. But I've overstayed my welcome."

Before Cassius could shoot the man where he stood, Lenin turned and fled from an entire group of chattering, jerking figures that stalked upon the concrete below them. The soldier followed the vagrant survivor across the skeletal remains of dusty buildings that had fallen or burned years ago.

Cassius and Lenin were forced to drop onto an open boulevard. A legion of hungry, listless dead pushed through the refuse. Some of them collided with one another, while others tripped out of doorways or slid out of windows.

The soldier knelt and squeezed the trigger on his submachine gun. He swept the flashing barrel over the shoulder blades of a collected group of lingering corpses, and each of them fell while stray bullets tickled their corrupt bodies.

There was no battle-high for the veteran. No rapid heartbeat or shortness of breath, no sense of elation or victory. It was more a nuisance for him; he hated to waste ammunition so early in a mission.

While more corpses collected in the street, Cassius leaned the smoking barrel of his gun beneath Lenin's chin. "I'm done playing games. You'll give me answers."

Lenin didn't seem intimidated by the weapon at all. Instead, he placed his index finger on the gun and eased it away from his face. "Of course. First, you should know that I'm the only one left alive. It's been that way for a few months. There's no intel on this place because nobody leaves. That's part of the reason why I like it here. You want to reach your goal, you need me. I know where it might be."

The legendary helmet, the object or rampant speculation throughout the living world. It was supposedly designed by the same people who designed the biological menace that brought the dead back to life.

The helmet was supposed to forge a connection between a living mind and the still-functioning brains of the Forsaken, a powerful legion of undead creatures that were crafted within underground laboratories.

Cassius didn't like Lenin's answer. But what choice did he have? He wasn't ready to buy the idea that this loner was the only one left in the town, considering that Springfield had been a popular survivor destination outside of New York because it was a merchant town.

But information from the mission briefing had been sketchy, though it bothered him that Lenin knew just as much about the mission that he did.

Staying alive wasn't a priority. It was his last job, after all. Men like him didn't retire. Even though New York's government had been giving out land grants to veteran soldiers left and right, just as the ancient Romans once did to ensure the loyalty of their troops, Cassius fled from inertia and straight into the wastelands. War was in his blood. It was his escape from the horrors that he'd witnessed in the first days.

The corpses groaned as they approached, stretching out their cracking limbs while their worked their fleshless jaws, grinding bone as decaying teeth dropped out of their mouths, pushed by active tongues.

Cassius slapped a fresh clip into his gun and once again swept his wrath over the desiccated caricatures of the living.

"We'll walk and talk," Lenin suggested. "You'll find exactly what you're looking for."

They traveled through a labyrinth of alleys and garbage, picking off the benevolent dead as they came within reaching distance.

"In the beginning," Lenin said, "this place was surrounded on all sides by a wall. I'm sure you've heard of it. Well, a particular blond man had the wall built. Maybe you've heard of...Harold?"

Cassius sneered. "I was in New York when everything started. I helped clean up the Empire State Building."

"The blond man, Harold," Lenin continued. "Everything he does is a twisted social experiment. I've seen what he can do to people out in the wasteland. I've seen entire cities, like Springfield, used in his projects. You've lived in New York, you know what that's like."

The soldier shrugged. "They have their way of doing things, there. Anyway, Harold's dead."

Lenin flinched visibly. "It doesn't matter if he is or isn't. Springfield is his creation."

Cassius was already growing bored with Lenin's explanation. "You've been to New York, yourself. You called those bastards unfriendlies—that's a New York military term."

"As I was saying," Lenin pressed. "Springfield was always a military curiosity, even before the shit hit the fan. The city was a test site for experimental chemicals, and not many people knew about it. They didn't know what was beneath their city, either.

"When the dead woke up, Harold ordered in a unit of his men to Springfield and they began to build a wall around the city. It was supposed to become a vacation spot or a retirement community. Nobody really knows for sure. But after they built the walls, someone was ordered to go beneath the city."

Lenin let his words hang in the air for a moment. "Do you even know what it is that you're looking for?"

"I know enough," Cassius spat.

Lenin shook his head. "Then you know about the Forsaken."

The specialized creatures that were genetically engineered in hidden labs all across the former country, manufactured somehow through Harold's grand design. It was Harold who brought the dead back to life with his biological weapon, and his desire to play god at the expense of the human race involved the creation of a super-corpse.

Cassius had his own share of combat experiences against those terrible monstrosities. No amount of preparation could possibly help against such pure savagery. The Forsaken loved murder for murder's sake, and were able to wield weapons and follow orders. They were an army of walking corpses, though nobody ever learned who commanded them, or what their true purpose was.

And this is why people believed that the helmet existed.

"They're all dead," Cassius said.

"Rumors." Lenin shook his head. "You're thinking about the battle in New York where the army found a base. That wasn't all of them. I was there when that happened."

Lenin's eyes seemed to grow large for a moment, and he stopped against a broken wall. The sun's light poured over the ashen street, and Cassius briefly covered his eyes as wind picked up the apocalyptic dust.

"So where are they?" Cassius asked.

Lenin snapped back to reality. A placid hand dropped onto his shoulder, and he turned around to find himself staring into the blackened maw of a creaking, lumbering corpse. When he pushed the creature away for Cassius to take his shot, he immediately threw his hood over the side of his face to prevent the stray bone fragments from its exploded skull from hitting him the face. It was a wise move.

"The Forsaken have been cleaned out," Lenin easily said as if his life hadn't been threatened at all. "But this place turned into a tourist trap for people looking to find the object. Then, it evolved into a trading outpost, and when the company-sponsored soldiers started to show up, they were all wiped out. Everybody eventually left. This thing you're looking for...you don't really want it."

"I want it," Cassius corrected him. "My sister came here for it. She led the first team in. Harold ordered her in himself, before the emperor came to power in New York."

Lenin nodded to himself and furrowed his brow. "That was a long time ago. The first team died, like all the others. What's your sister's name?"

"What difference does it make? Are we going to stand around here?"

Lenin smiled and returned his attention to the street. While the cloud cover above them thickened, the sun was lost behind an impending storm. Another gust of wind shifted the swaying bushes and leaves that jutted out from behind the ghostly city.

An inhalation of fetid breath carried by the wind reminded Cassius of a dying old man whose body had already given up. The soldier had long ago vowed that he would never die that way, that his end would be on the battlefield against the foul creatures that claimed his sister's life, long ago. She'd been a member of the only team New York ever sent into the doomed city.

But he was in Springfield now, at last. He'd been running from this moment for years. He could have gone in with a team at any point during his career, but he'd always stayed away.

The undead never ceased or desisted in their desire for human flesh. They crawled over shattered cars and seemed to linger on the edges of perception. They were the nightmarish monsters that haunted the realm of the living, carnivorously eating away at the remaining threads of sanity that forever scarred those who'd survived. Safe behind walls in New York or within a secluded mountain retreat, the dead would never go away. There was no cure for death.

They appeared from around corners, their shambling multitude a featureless assembly of shapes. With phlegmatic groans and heavy-lidded eyes, they shifted their universe upon the living. They'd lingered within the glimpses of fear their terrible presence represented. Any flesh that remained was shriveled and almost colorless, their entire forms a mess of black, gray, and faded blue. Any clothes that hadn't been looted from them long ago hung in threadbare pieces along the slack, withered muscle tissue and shriveled organs that sometimes fell from exposed stomachs, or slipping against the bone. They were a collection of pieces. Their heads turned only with great effort, and they carried with them a retinue of creeping insects. They stretched out their arms for the two survivors as if chasing a hug.

Lenin stayed out of the way while Cassius worked, mowing down entire swaths and mobs. Cassius moved like an expert craftsman while the other simply waited as if he could escape at any moment. He forced the soldier to expend precious ammunition, a resource that would have been valuable had Lenin any designs on stealing it.

He began to feel detached from the exercise. It was as if the dead were nothing more than obstacles in his path to something far more powerful, something with the revelatory power to change a man's soul. Where was the sense of glory, the rush of knowing that one was alive? Where was the old bloodlust? He was eliminating scores of unfriendlies, yet, it was becoming difficult for him to differentiate each confrontation from the last. He noticed only the dwindling supply of ammunition. He would have to switch to the handguns soon.

This moment had been years in the making.

Lenin ritualistically stopped to pick his way through the corpses, while Cassius simply watched and waited. His patience began to wear thin. Not all of his questions had been answered.

"What're you looking for?" Cassius finally asked. "How many have we brought down? Maybe if we move faster."

"It won't make a difference," Lenin said. "I want the same things you want. They've tried to repopulate this place so many times, but nobody knows why it doesn't...grow back. We often think that Harold is done with us, that he's finally gone and we don't have to worry about another vile experiment. We thought he was done with Springfield."

"Where the hell is the helmet?" Cassius drew one of his pistols.

"This is the closest you've ever been," Lenin said. "Was it worth it to be a soldier? Is there a difference between us?"

"I won't ask again."

"You're right about that. You'll find the entrance inside the court house. I know it sounds like a joke, but I think it's supposed to be one of Harold's attempts to use a metaphor."

"Why wouldn't you have it yourself, if you know where it is?"

"I never said I didn't have it."

A flood of unfriendlies suddenly began to pour between two collapsed houses, crushing weeds beneath their feet and stumbling through piles of broken brick. They pushed over a fence and crowded around a child's plastic playhouse, the little red plastic door swinging back and forth on its hinges beneath a blue roof. Together they seemed like a forest of falling trees, their bones cracking and breaking, their agonizing groans adding an electric hum.

Lenin slipped away while Cassius held both pistols in his hands and took aim as quickly as he could. Backing up, he squeezed off a series of rounds, putting two down, but there were too many. The entire tide of dead would wash over him.

He needed high ground. He fled into a brick home that still stood upright, pushing past two corpses that were in his way. He climbed up a flight of stairs, crawled out of a bedroom window, reached up to the roof with his fingers, and pulled himself out, stretching tendons and burning his shoulder with fiery pain.

On the roof, he carefully took aim at the swarm. The crowd never thinned, no matter how many he seemed to drop. He worked quickly, racing from one end of the roof to the other, sweat pouring into his eyes. He stopped to reload, and resumed bringing a final, ultimate destruction upon those horrendous creatures.

He felt invincible. He was the living embodiment of Death, a gracious being that willingly bestowed its gift upon the wall of greedy dead. It was a moment he'd always envisioned for himself. It was as if every single one of them, from all across the silent world, converged upon him, lusting for his flesh.

Bring them all. Bring every one of them.

Another reload. A group of corpses had piled on top of one another, and it was easy for an ambitious unfriendly to reach up and grab the soldier's ankle while his attention was focused on the guns. He'd come too close to the edge. In all the excitement, he'd unraveled his methodical, machine-like techniques.

He instantly lost his footing and one of the guns fled from his fingers. He fell and twisted himself through their fragile arms. He hadn't been able to reload the other gun, but he held it tightly in his other hand.

He'd been bitten before, but not where he couldn't see it. The incredibly quick flash of hot pain that burned through his left ankle nearly caused him to cry out. Who would hear his scream? Lenin? Where was that man? Why did he go through all the trouble of leading him through the city, if all he ever wanted was the loot from his own corpse? Why would he let Cassius burn through ammo?

Nina. Did she die the same way, with visions of her own final stand dancing within her head? The creatures had been quicker then, and most of them would have still resembled living people.

No. The living dead were a biological condition rather than the result of an infectious contagion, a concept Cassius had been familiar with in popular fiction before the dead became a reality. When another chunk of his flesh was ripped away from his shoulder, it was all he could to reach and push with the last reserves of his fleeting strength.

He dropped to his knees beneath a canopy of leering mouths and twitching arms. He crawled and ignored every stab of pain that filled his head with warmth. He could keep going. There was no need to give up. A powerful silence had been broken within him. A barrage of familiar voices accused him of giving up, of letting his country down.

But he'd given everything for the government that betrayed him, that sold him to a scientist who was going to wipe out the human race. Everyone had always been so proud of Nina, but her relationship to her brother had always been a fragile one. She'd always been so strong and prideful, so resolute in her beliefs. She was upset when she couldn't fight on the front lines, but it was always her wish to be the first to defend the United States, no matter where she needed to fight. She went to church every Sunday, and was a devout Republican.

When he saw her in New York, she believed that she was still defending America, that democracy and freedom were eternal concepts. They could never die, she said, so our country can never die.

He crawled until he was able to stand among them. Cassius pushed his way through them, and struggled to load his last gun. He dropped the submachine gun to the ground and shouted, "Here it is, Lenin! Isn't this what you want?"

The skull mask had been ripped away from his neck, along with the chain. He'd found a break in the crowd, and favored his bleeding shoulder. He needed to be able to stop and make a tourniquet for his arm, somehow staunch the bleeding.

The corpses swam in his vision. He steadied himself and dragged his wounded body away from the crowd, leaning heavily against a wall.

He almost stopped himself with an uncharacteristic, melancholy question: what had been the point of it all, to end this way?

He was a soldier. It was the only thing he needed to be.

"Where's your extraction point?" Lenin's voice called out from across the rooftops above.

Cassius stopped for a moment. Only a few feet behind him were the shambling dead. They were zombies, creatures that were once common images incorporated into popular culture. A subconscious hunger for human flesh, perpetuated by a mob mentality, urged them forward.

He desperately wanted a shot at Lenin. He kept one finger on the trigger of the gun. If he died, he would be one of them. If he bled to death, he would come back. When should he end it for himself? What was the difference?

The mission could still be completed.

The wounds could still get infected, or he could go into shock. Time was against him. He couldn't call for extraction if he didn't have the object. They were likely going to shoot him on sight, anyway.

So what was the point? His death wish had brought him face-to-face with his end. The mission was always going to be impossible.

When Nina disappeared into Springfield, Cassius became restless. He preferred to be a roving spirit rather than a revolutionary soldier. Everything he'd once loved and cared about disappeared with her. His sense of reality finally surrendered.

The horde chased after him, and it was what he ultimately desired, more than anything.

He charged for a wide road that stood desolate beneath a still-standing set of traffic lights. The clouds were a shifting, swirling mass of gunmetal, and the wind passed furiously, rifling the ridges of the soldier's hair. Thunder shook the horizon, overriding the moaning which doggedly hounded him. There was no escape.

He pivoted once and turned, kneeling again to take precise aim. He would have to thin them out before attempting to spread them out. He wouldn't have a chance in all that open space. He quickly dropped one, then a second, and a third. The creatures crowded into another, creating a bottleneck. Cassius rose to his feet and picked several of them off.

The pain was incredible. Now, at last, his heart joined the fight. It fluttered within his chest, and a rush of joy seemed to define his love for battle. There were moments left to him. Why not enjoy it?

The last bullet was spent. It was decided, then. He drew the bat again and took a deep breath, angry with himself for smoking.

He blasted one skull with a tremendous swing. They needed him, as if their ghoulish fate was dependent on their ability to open up his chest cavity and scoop his innards into their mouths. He swung again and brought a corpse down with one crack. With a surge of strength, he brought the bat down atop the head of another, and the creature folded beneath his strike.

Breathing raggedly, he brought down a fourth creature and backed into the boulevard. He turned and limped across the street. They were still coming, coalescing out of leaning houses and from open garages. They slid out from beneath cars. They wanted him. They wanted all of him.

Cassius bled across the pavement but steadily passed beneath the tremulous storm clouds. He felt enclosed. Despite the vast stretches of nothing in either direction, running was useless. They seemed to materialize out of thin air. Hundreds of them simply wandered in his direction. The dead seemed to have been waiting for him, as if he was a benign prophet or a celebrated actor.

The courthouse. If Lenin told the truth, the mythical helmet for which men had given their lives resided within. How did so many others lose their lives in that place, whereas Cassius, nearly alone, was able to struggle his way across the city? Did the helmet's location remain a mystery to them, or was Cassius simply that good?

He quickly pushed his way into the surprisingly-intact courthouse. Cassius staggered through the creaking doors while an onslaught of dust and cobwebs barred his path. Lenin had mentioned an entrance...where could it be? An entrance to what?

Thunder shook the sky as the soldier frantically stepped over headless skeletons cocooned in dust and made his way toward the basement. Lenin had mentioned something about an underground facility. He'd rambled on about Springfield operating as a test site for Forsaken, the vicious killing machines that wrecked havoc on the sheltered cities. Did they guard the helmet?

In the dust-laden gloom, he staggered his way down a dark stairwell, feeling the wall and easing himself downward. The bat was his only remaining weapon. He never expected the mission to begin and end so quickly, nor did he anticipate that he would go through so much ammo.

It was his last mission, live or die.

He didn't get far when a sudden conflagration of lights erupted around him, filling the stairwell with light. The entire courthouse hummed, and another explosion of thunder vibrated the walls while dust rained into his eyes. It was real. The helmet was close.

Another set of doors. Who'd built this place? What was its purpose? Why was it hidden in plain sight? Cassius could only wonder about the world that had passed—all of its mysteries were no longer significant. Whatever Harold intended with his maniacal experiments, the city eventually became a killing ground.

Cassius, broken and bleeding, his mouth parched, opened the final set of doors. Black spots were sprinkled into his vision, while his confused mind raced with a myriad of visions and ideas. At long last, a welcome rush of warmth filled him, as if he'd never understood what it meant to be happy until that moment.

Rows of ceiling lights flickered on once the doors were open. A tombstone chill wafted from out of the large, narrow chamber. Large, cylindrical tubes were attached to banks of flickering computer monitors. He felt as if he here were stepping into a frigid, ominous tomb.

Most of the large tubes were empty. Row after row of those strange devices were lined up across the vibrant facility.

He stopped at the lone tube that wasn't empty. Floating within a viscous, bubbling liquid, was a nude woman seemingly frozen in a fetal pose. Various tubes and wires had been injected into her pale flesh.

"No," Cassius shook his head. It couldn't be. Nina was dead. That couldn't be her, the victim of some horrifying science project. But it seemed just like her...

He shook his head. If she'd been captured during her mission, then maybe they intended to use her as a Forsaken. Harold, the enterprising scientist with the Dystopian vision, had taken everything Cassius had ever loved, and everything his sister cared about.

With his finger hovering above the console, he quickly pushed a series of random buttons and controls. He hardly paused to read the prompts on the screen. He had to find a way to release her.

The liquid in the tube began to drain.

A sharp, burning pain arched its way up from the small of his back. He'd been so foolish to think he wouldn't be followed. After everything he'd been through, everything he'd suffered...

Lenin stood behind him, holding a bloody knife. Cassius collapsed and stared upward at the dusty survivor. He understood at last why Lenin preferred the edged weapons.

"Baseball bat," Lenin pointed. "That's all you have for trade. You're lucky, you know. I could have twisted the knife a little."

Cassius had a difficult time mustering the strength to speak. The underground lab seemed colder.

"The helmet," Cassius managed.

Lenin shrugged. "A helmet that can give someone the power to speak to the dead? To command them? Never seen it. Springfield was a test city for the Forsaken. They butchered everyone in this place. This is where they were grown. Of course, Harold tried to use it again."

Cassius focused his attention on the nude woman in the tube. The body slumped forward against the glass. She looked so much like Nina. Would she have been proud of him?

Lenin knelt near a console and withdrew a large box from within his robe, something he'd been carrying with him the entire time. Cassius recognized it as C4. Lenin was going to blow the place up.

The figure in the tube slowly moved a hand and removed one of the wires imbedded in its flesh.

Cassius swallowed. None of his muscles responded. Lenin stood over him holding the baseball bat.

Shattering glass rained onto the soldier's slow-rising chest.

Lenin smiled. "A lot of people died for this to happen, including you. You're a hero. There won't be any more Forsaken coming out of this place, thanks to you."

Deep, swirling black eyes peered into the dying soldier's face. He said her name, and the nude monster stretched and emitted a terrible roar.

For the first time since it all started, Cassius replied with a terrified scream.

ZOMBIE WALK

JOSEPH DUMAS

A mass of undead stumbled together to meet their leader in the center of town. Amongst the group was Jamie. He had seen a few of Romero's finest, but was definitely not a zombie-nut like the rest of the people there.

At the beginning of the tenth grade, he'd met Charlotte. She was in his study hall and was always drawing and doodling pictures of things like zombies and evil clowns. It didn't bother him too much, but he never expected to be friends—or more—with her. Eventually, they began to talk to one another. She asked him questions about movies that he'd seen. One day she insisted they hang out after school and watch the 1968 classic, *Night of the Living Dead.*

Jamie never had a girlfriend, so he was more than willing to step outside his comfort zone to impress her. They met at Jamie's house and enjoyed some snack food and watched the movie. Jamie actually liked it and they eventually agreed to watch another soon. This continued for weeks until one day Charlotte arrived at his house with a flyer in her hand.

3RD ANNUAL ZOMBIE WALK – COME PREPARED TO EAT BRAAAINS

Jamie looked at the flyer in amazement that such an event actually existed. He knew immediately Charlotte would ask him to go with him.

"We have to go!" she said. "You have to be at least sixteen to participate and this year I'll finally be old enough."

"Okay, what do we do?"

"Easy, we dress up like zombies. Blood, guts, brains, all the good stuff!"

Jamie smiled reluctantly and agreed to give it a shot.

Soon, the day arrived. Jamie was dressed in a *'blood'*-stained dress shirt and slacks. Charlotte was looking the same, just in a formerly-white dress—now pinkish red from all the corn syrup-based blood. She'd come up with the look and said they could go as an undead bride and groom. Jamie had agreed because surely *that* meant she liked him.

As the horde of 'zombies' gathered in the center of town, they congregated around a stone wall that stood about six feet tall. Atop the wall stood a man dressed in full zombie garb. He'd gone to the trouble to even apply latex with makeup to create a flap of skin falling from his cheek bone. If Jamie had seen this man on a more average day, he'd have probably run away as fast as possible. The horrid-looking leader stood tall and proud as his blood-soaked arms were raised and he lifted a megaphone to his mouth.

"Ladies and gents!" he said proudly. "Thank you for coming to the Third Annual Zombie Walk! We have a record turnout today of…"

As he spoke about the walk, Jamie looked around at the zombie faces that filled the crowd. As he scanned, he noticed a police presence at the perimeter of the group. Beyond them, he spotted civilian spectators and even a news crew. Between Channel 5 and the dozens of smartphones, there must've been twenty or more cameras on the zombie walkers. This made Jamie a little anxious to the point that Charlotte noticed and asked him if he was okay. Jamie shrugged off the question at first and attempted to play it cool, that is until his eyes caught up with a police officer holding a nightstick in his right hand and slapping it gently into his left palm.

Jamie cleared his throat and asked, "What's with the cops?"

"Don't worry," she said. "We're a big crowd, and they just have to be here in case anything happens."

"What could happen?" he asked.

"Ha-ha, *what* could happen?"

"So, that being said, let's have a fun time and eat plenty of braaaainssss!" the zombie leader said, ending with a roar from the undead-loving crowd of movie and video game buffs…and Jamie.

The leader jumped off the wall and began stumbling like a true zombie, moaning and groaning like mad. As he stumbled, the crowd let out massive moans that echoed through the small, downtown shops. The walk was on and the crowd began moving down the road. Onlookers continued taking photos and video of the display.

As the crowd began to walk, Jamie's anxiety went away as he and Charlotte blended right in. Jamie and Charlotte walked with stiff legs and moaned like something out of the movies. He couldn't help but laugh with enjoyment.

"Don't make me bite you!" she laughed, smiling at him through her grim makeup.

"Sorry!"

Agghh Aggggghhh!

The sound came from in front of them and stuck out from the monotonous moans of the wannabe zombies. As Jamie looked ahead, he spotted a man keeled over, puking up at least two full meals, followed closely by blood.

"Uh man, gross, are you okay?" Charlotte asked as she covered her nose and mouth.

Jamie looked away, closing his eyes in disgust.

The man looked up at Charlotte with a blank stare. He looked terrible—but who didn't in this mass of 'undead'? He reached for her and let out a raspy moan.

"Very funny," she said, "Really, are you okay?"

With no response, the man moved towards her as Jamie looked on and gave a small smirk at the man's zombie passion.

Charlotte continued to laugh and pointed away from her, "Come on, Jamie," she said. "The march is going that way."

"Some people really take this stuff seriously, huh?" he said.

Charlotte nodded as the seemingly drunk zombie grabbed her arms.

"Come on!" Charlotte shouted as other zombie fans looked at her.

"Take it easy," Jamie said.

The seemingly real zombie sunk his teeth into Charlotte's bicep as she cried for help. Jamie pushed the man off of her and shouted, "That's not funny! What the hell are you doing?"

"Take it easy man," another person said.

Charlotte fell to the ground as blood ran from her arm. She grabbed onto Jamie's pant leg.

He crouched down and consoled her. "Somebody get help!" he shouted.

Two policemen perked up at the cry for help, but weren't able to find the source amongst all of the walking zombies. A few of them began moving into the crowd until one saw the gruesome sight.

"What happened to her?" the police officer asked.

"She was bit!" Jamie said frantically.

"Very funny, kid…" he said and began to turn away, annoyed at the situation.

Then, the sick man lunged at Jamie and bit into his arm. Jamie tried to fight him off but couldn't do it.

"Help!" Jamie screamed again.

"Damn it," the cop said as he turned back to Jamie, "Listen kid I…"

He stopped when he saw the man tear through Jamie's flesh.

"Damn it!"

Clutching his pepper spray, he ran at them. "Shut your eyes, kid!"

Jamie listened and the cop unleashed the brutal spray onto the man. Unaffected, the man continued feasting on Jamie. However, the tight crowd all gagged at the spray as it reached those nearby. Two other zombie walkers tackled the cop in fury. Anarchy of an unknown caliber broke out and Jamie wasn't sure if the mob was angry or infected like the man on top of him.

Charlotte, gagging on the spray, pushed the man away from her and grabbed onto Jamie. She planted a kiss on his cheek and said, "I never should've brought you here."

Gunshots emanated throughout the crowd as the police attempted to maintain order. Jamie looked at the police firing the weapons and watched as another seemingly infected person or zombie attacked one of them. The cop fell to the ground as the grotesque looking fiend bit into his neck. Jamie then watched as others ran to some onlookers wielding smart phones and did the same to them. *Were these real zombies*? Jamie began to wonder *Or are these people just being passionate*?

He received his answer a second later when two zombies tackled him and began tearing into his stomach, pulling out his insides. Nearby, he could hear Charlotte screaming as the same was done to her.

Soon, the *fake* zombies had become what they were mimicking. As one massive undead crowd, they made their way into the city.

ROTTING FLESH LOVE STORY

T. FOX DUNHAM

Liana ground the soaked shirt against the washboard, working in the dim, predawn light. They didn't do chores during the day, too much of a chance of stirring up the undead. The cool night had a soporific effect on the undead. They mostly just stumbled about in circles, biting at fireflies, looked almost peaceful.

Hilda and Chuck both sat on a towel on the kitchen floor, twisting the wet clothing, then securing it to the improvised clothesline they had strung across the kitchen. Chuck paused between each shirt to plant a quick kiss on Hilda. Chuck grinned. Hilda giggled. Liana clutched the washing board, ready to smack Hilda across her head.

"Should have left her to the wormheads," Liana muttered beneath the scrubbing sound of the washboard.

They leaned in for a longer kiss. Liana raked the board and split her fingernail. Blood stained the soapy water.

"Get a room," she said. She examined her finger and searched the cabinet drawer for a Band-Aid.

Chuck took off his old t-shirt, revealing the skull and roses arrangements on his pecs and shoulder. Liana couldn't breathe, her chest tightening. He pulled a shirt from a dry laundry batch off the line and put it on. He winked at Hilda. She giggled, and he extended her hand to help her up.

"Let's make the best of our last bit of the morning, Peaches," he said.

She giggled again. Liana swung the washboard in a mock strike on Hilda's temple. Hilda took Chuck's hand and followed him into the bedroom on the other side of the one-story rancher.

She wasn't going to cry. Damn it. She wasn't going to sob like some weak little girl, powerless and pathetic. She lobbed the washboard into the boards nailed over the window sink. It knocked two of them free. They clattered into the sink, echoing through the silent suburb of Lansdale. Two zombies heard it, the sound like she was ringing a dinner gong. She watched them through the kitchen window, stumbling across the front garden. The right one reminded her of George Bush Jr. It was dressed in a sodden, navy-blue suit, accessorized by the gouge bitten out of its gray neck. The other zombie's belly jiggled as it walked, skin bags of water dangling under its skin and down its sagging abdomen.

She grabbed the boards and the hammer from a drawer. It didn't matter though. The zombies had seen her with their bloated, leaking eyes, which were wide now, like a hunting predator. They'd never stop now, single-minded and free of fatigue in their purpose, now that they knew a feast of warm flesh could be found inside the house.

Perhaps she could bust in Hilda's skull with the hammer. The thought of the spraying blood nauseated Liana. She'd thought about poisoning her Spam, but there wasn't anything effective left in the house. She'd looked around some of the stores during their last supply run, but most everything had been ruined after a flash flood had hit the town.

She pressed the first board to the window and tapped lightly, driving the nails into the soft drywall with little noise. The zombies groaned, shambling into reach. She heard one of their ankles snap. The zombie dragged its foot behind it on the lawn, leaving a yellow ooze in the uncut grass.

She propped up the second board.

For the last two months, it was just Liana and Chuck. They'd been roommates before the Helsinki-221 Virus transformed from miracle remedy for cancer to the cure for the common death.

They'd lived together for the last four years in the Levittown rancher, orbiting in separate circles. She'd never been attractive and was never able to shed the couple of extra pounds that had inspired her last boyfriend to give her the nickname 'Chunky.' It wasn't until society fell apart that they finally noticed each other, exploding with the need for human contact. Love may not have been their motivation, but she found being with him satisfying.

She tapped the nail for the second board and secured it in place, while swallowing back vomit after smelling the rancid odor of rotting flesh seeping in from outside. The bulbous zombie with the sagging bags of flesh screeched and flailed against the reinforced window. She scanned the yard, expecting to see a mob of zombies. There must have been a stray dog running through the neighborhood, because only the two were attacking the house. Two were manageable.

They had found Hilda hiding in the meat freezers of the Piggly Wiggly on their first supply run. She didn't speak for four days after joining them. Chuck made her his special project, to bring her back to sanity.

Liana could see the immediate bond between them, something in the way they looked at one another. Finally, Chuck had found something with slim hips and a bit of cleavage, just how he liked it. He didn't need to play with Liana anymore. He had a new doll.

She just had to figure out a way of killing Hilda so that Chuck wouldn't suspect her, one that wouldn't be so obvious, or he would never forgive her. George Bush and Bags clawed at the window. Bush stumbled in the rose beds, lost his footing, and collapsed. Decomposition slowed the zombies. She could handle them by herself.

She ran into the living room, down the back hall, and pushed open the bedroom door. Chuck and Hilda were rolling around in the bed, wrapped in flannel sheets.

"Two of them broke in," she said flatly.

Chuck jumped from the bed, naked, exposing the tattoos of roses down his flat stomach. Hilda shook her head, clenching a clump of sheet to hide her nakedness. Both of them were covered in sweat from their exertions.

"Chuck, I heard them breaking down the backdoor. Sounded like maybe five or more."

"Saint Chris, protect us," he whispered. He didn't stop to put on some jeans, and grabbed his M-1 off the dresser and checked to make sure it was loaded.

"Hilda, I need you in the kitchen. They're about to break down the door."

Hilda picked up a pair of shorts and a tank top from the floor. She dressed under the sheet. She paused to tie up her hair and Liana shook her head. Zombies could be breaking into the house to devour their warm flesh, but Hilda had to make sure that her hair looked good. She actually paused in front of the mirror to check, and even reached for a brush.

"Damn it, girl," Liana hissed impatiently. "Are you waiting for room service?"

Hilda dropped the brush and it banged on the dresser. Chuck had his rifle loaded and ran to the backdoor. Hilda followed Liana to the kitchen. Liana darted ahead and unlocked the kitchen door, pulling it free from the flimsy nails in the dry, rotted wood. The two zombies had long since pulled down the screen door.

Bush and Bags wobbled through the doorway. Liana stepped aside. The undead always went for the first sighted prey.

Before she knew what was happening, the zombies were tackling Hilda. Bush bit a bloody chunk out of her shoulder and warm blood sprayed onto the kitchen floor. Hilda screamed so high that it cracked a crystal pitcher on top of the cabinet. Damn, that girl had opera-singer lungs, Liana thought.

Chuck charged into the kitchen, aiming his M-1.

"Jesus Christ," he yelled. "Baby!"

He fired, the bullet going through Bush's cheek. The body dropped, the animation gone. He turned to take down Bags, but the bloated zombie charged him like a quarterback, knocking him into the cabinets. They snapped the clothesline, and wet shirts and jeans spilled onto the table and floor. Bags chewed into Chuck's shoulder, ripping flesh from his neck. Chuck fired but missed, the bullet becoming buried in the ceiling.

"No, not that one," Liana said angrily and pulled Bags off of Chuck.

He aimed his rifle at the zombie. "Get out of the way!" he yelled.

He took the zombie down with a shot through the forehead, then dropped the rifle and slid to the floor. Liana knelt beside him, pressing her hands to the wound in his neck, but she couldn't stop the blood pouring. It poured down her arms and chest. His carotid artery had been torn.

"I'm so sorry, Chuck. I just wanted you back. I just wanted…"

His head dropped to the side. His body slid down further to the floor, catching on the cabinet handles. Hilda gazed up at the ceiling.

He stopped breathing.

Liana began to cry. She screeched like a little girl and pounded her fists on the cabinet next to Chuck's head.

A nearby growl from Hilda suddenly shocked her out of her grief. She gathered herself quickly, knowing her life was in danger, and reached for the rifle. Now they *both* had to be put down. She aimed and shot Hilda through her left ear. The bullet split her jaw and exited out the other side, lodging in the wall amidst bone fragments and blood.

All the noise had attracted more zombies. The undead lumbered through the kitchen doorway, snapping their jaws in anticipation of feeding.

Liana aimed the rifle at Chuck's head just as he twitched, the first sparks of reanimation firing off in his brain. She squeezed the trigger slightly, but not enough, unable to summon the strength to fire the rifle.

She'd always had to sacrifice for love, being chubby and without the looks of a runway model. She'd always had to accept it when her boyfriends had cheated on her or just would ignore her for days before she finally phoned them to plead for a little attention. Even at the end of the world, nothing had changed for her.

She stood up and stretched her arm out, offering it to the lead zombie, a kid. It bit into her arm right to the bone. She bit her tongue, trying not to scream. Salty blood pooled in her mouth.

Sliding down the back of the cabinet, she took Chuck's hand in hers. It flexed to her touch, animation returning. Liana pointed the gun at her chest and fired. Blood filling her throat, choking her, it became her last, living sensation. In a moment, she'd care neither for pain or love.

Two zombies stumbled down Thornridge Drive, the male dragging the female. Their hands were locked in a tight grip from the rigor mortis. They would never let go. They chased after a fleeing dog, among a pack of other zombies.

The couple would never be apart now. They would stay in love for as long as their rotting flesh held together.

THE WATCHER

ANTHONY GIANGREGORIO

I awoke to the sound of screaming.

Jumping up from the couch I was sleeping on, I dashed across the floor to one of the boarded-up windows that overlooked the street and the front yard of my house. My growling stomach made me wince but I ignored it. There would be time to eat later, but right now I needed to know who on my street was getting it next.

It was Sam Rodriquez, my neighbor from across the street. Only it looked like he wasn't going to be my neighbor for much longer.

In about ten seconds he was going to become zombie chow.

There were about twenty zombies, maybe more, gathered around the front of Sam's house. It was hard to count them as they shifted back and forth, constantly moving. They reminded me of waves on a beach, ebbing and flowing, undulating. It was almost hypnotic.

I saw some faces I recognized in the undead crowd. People I'd seen at the park or when I was at the grocery store. Not that I went anywhere now. No one did.

It had been months since the dead first started walking, when cadavers climbed off cold steel tables to attack coroners, or after dying in a car accident. Those paramedics must have gotten a hell of a shock when they went to a fallen man or women only to have that person sit up and take a bite out of the care giver that had arrived to help them.

Huh, it was kind of clichéd I suppose. I mean, anyone who had ever watched a zombie movie knows what happens when some-one dies and another goes to help that person. Closed eyes will pop open and pupils will slide from left to right as the helper tries to see how bad the wounds are. Then the mouth opens and *chomp*, the carnage begins.

Well, sometimes life imitates art and that's what happened a few months ago.

Believe me I get it. Right now you're reading this and rolling your eyes, saying how this story sounds like a million others you may have read back when books were still getting made. Well, I have something to tell you. I don't care. See, this is my story, this is my life, and though it may sound repetitive to you, to me it matters. So if you don't like it then stop reading now because I plan on telling the entire story. Funny how people like to try and make a book or movie their own no matter what. Hell, a guy could write a story about, oh I don't know, say a book about killer rats. But hold on, if someone else wrote one forty years ago, than you know some asshole out there is going to complain. How dare that guy write a book about the same thing. It didn't seem to matter that when the first book came out the writer had been three years old. That's right. Three! And he probably couldn't even wipe his own ass yet let alone read a book, but then, forty years later and the writer gets an idea and someone remembers the first one, it's like, "Oh my God, how could someone else dare write a book about the same thing? One is enough in the world. We don't need two books about killer rats, that's insane!"

God, people are such assholes, aren't they? Maybe you're one, too, but I don't know you so I'll give you the benefit of the doubt.

See, I was a writer before the dead began to walk and guess what I wrote about? That's right, I wrote zombie novels. Ironic? Sure, it is. So if anyone can survive this shit it should be me. I watched zombie movies till my eyes bled, and written over twenty novels and a hell of a lot of short stories about the walking dead. I know them inside and out. But I have to be honest with you.

I can, can't I?

I mean, I don't know you but you seem like a nice person and it's not like I can tell you private stuff and later you're going to go on the internet and tell the world about it. You can't! There's no fucking internet. It's all gone! Like TV, phones and everything else. Dust in the fucking wind and all that shit.

I'm sure if I said the name George Romero you'd know who I'm talking about. If you don't, go back under the rock you've been living under because you don't know anything about zombies. Well, I wonder what happened to him when the dead began to walk. I bet he was one of the first to go. I can see it now: He's out in Canada now, you know. He gave the US the finger and went to live in Canada. Can't say I blame him much, most Americans are assholes.

So Romero's walking down his driveway to get his newspaper that the damn paperboy keeps tossing there instead of up on the porch and Romero bends over and picks it up, and when he does, he sees all these people walking towards him, all dressed like zombies. And you know what he does? He tells them: "Walk like you think a zombie should, folks, just do it your way." He has to say this cause if he holds his arms out and says to walk stiff, he'd have two dozen ghouls all walking the same way.

Only, it's not a zombie walk or a bunch of fans, it's the real damn thing, and as he stands there in his slippers and pajamas and his fly open, his bathrobe untied, he waits for them to get closer, hoping they have a pen for the autograph the crowd surely wants. But as they get closer, he fixes those massive eyeglasses the ones the size of Mars, and blinks as the first zombie gets close enough to make out details.

And just before they swarm him, he realizes this shit isn't acting and that he's about to have a really cool death scene in the movie that was his life. Shit, that would suck. He ends up dying in a zombie scene and he doesn't even get a dollar, a donut and a fucking t-shirt.

But I'm getting off track. I bet you want to know what's happening to my neighbor Sam. Okay, as I peered out my window, I saw that wasn't doing too well. The zombies had attacked en masse and five of the more spry ones managed to break down the front door as another group climbed through the windows after forcing their way through the wooden boards that had covered the windows.

Did I mention that Sam is an asshole? Oh yeah, I can't fucking stand him. He's in the military you know. Flies a helicopter. He thinks he's such a big shot. At all the block parties we used to have he would always be standing with most of the guys in the neighborhood, telling story after story, the men all hanging on his every word. But I know the truth about Sam. He was a backstabbing bastard who had the morals of a rat. Seriously, you couldn't tell him anything without him passing it along to everyone else. The man knew nothing of privacy, or respect for others.

He was a piece of shit, and as I watched the zombies pull him through a window and onto his front lawn, I have to say I was feeling pretty good about it.

Sam was screaming by this time and those screams soon turned to shrieks as more than a dozen hands began pawing at him, fingernails digging into his flesh. A few aspiring zombies tore into his abdomen after ripping off his shirt. In a matter of seconds, intestines were being pulled out and the ghouls were gnawing on them as if they were raw sausage links. I wondered if the greasy loops were spicy, as Sam was Spanish or Mexican or some such thing. You know how they all look alike? I wonder if they all taste alike? I'm kidding, I'm not a racist, or not much of one anyway. Brown, tan, it's all the fucking same to the zombies. Am I being a little prejudicial? Maybe, but it's the end of the fucking world, are you saying I still need to be politically correct, too? Screw you.

Okay, fine. Here, to make you feel better, I'm Polish, so I guess I'm pretty stupid. Hey, how many Polish guys does it take to put in a light bulb? Two. One to watch and the other to hold the bulb and turn around a circle. Happy? See, it doesn't matter what color you are. Black, white, yellow, it's all the same to the walking dead. To them, we're all just piles of warm meat they want to feed on. Dark meat, white meat, they don't care!

And that's the problem Sam is realizing as well as the rest of my neighbors as they watch from the windows of their homes.

See, back when it all began, we could have gotten together, tried to fight them, but we didn't. Instead, we all went our separate ways and holed up alone, with our families. Well, not me. I'm divorced and the bitch got the kids and I got the child support payments.

I hope my kids are okay but I hope that bitch of an ex-wife is getting eaten right now. That image keeps me warm at night when it gets cold, as there's no heat. My home was heated by gas and that stopped pumping more than a month ago.

Sam the asshole is done screaming by the way and he's now very dead. One arm has been torn off and the meat in both legs has been eaten. Man, there's a lot of blood on the grass.

And it happened just like I thought it would. The zombies began backing away from Sam and making a small circle around him.

Yup, Sam's back among us again, only this time he's a little lighter than before. He has no internal organs as they have all been torn out and eaten, and like I said, his legs were pretty messed up. But he got to his feet on these skeletons for legs.

I thought he was going to fall over once but he managed to regain his balance. Zombies are funny. They seem to always be able to stand up, despite serious damage to their bodies. Sam then wandered away, just one more dead soul among the crowd.

Poor Sam, not such a hot shit on the ground, are you? Not so tough when you're not in a helicopter.

Then there were four houses left untouched in the neighborhood.

There was me, the neighbors on both sides of me, and the house next to Sam.

We're all that's left of the neighborhood. All the other homes have been besieged and the occupants killed and eaten.

I know my turn will be one of these times but so far I've been lucky. If you can call living like this lucky. With the zombies fed for the moment, they began moving away and it will be quiet for at least a few hours before they become restless again.

I'm going to try and get some more sleep and then I'll write some more. I like writing about this, what I've seen and experienced. Hey, maybe someone will find my manuscript one day if the world gets back to normal and I'll become a bestseller when they publish it.

If so, I hereby give anyone who finds this manuscript permission to publish it. Just make sure to use my whole name please. I want the name William Masters on the cover right below the name of the book.

At least there aren't any fucking e-books around anymore. I can't stand those damn things. You know how much use you get out of a kindle when the battery runs out and there's no power to charge it? Nothing, that's what.

At least if I'm done with a book made out of paper I can use the pages as toilet paper or as kindling for a fire. What can you do with a kindle? Nothing.

Well, maybe use it as a small plate to eat off of I suppose, or a Frisbee.

But that's it. The damn thing is worthless. I'm tired, I'm going to sleep.

Gunshots woke me this time and when I checked my wristwatch, I saw that I'd slept for most of the day. With the house boarded up, not much light manages to penetrate the windows, and whether it was day or night soon became irrelevant.

Once more I went to the window overlooking the street to see that the zombies were at it again. This time they were attacking the house next to Sam's.

The Robbins family lived there.

There was Tim, Susan and their two kids, Mike and Nancy, each child around seven or eight. I could hear their kids screaming as the zombies broke down the door and poured into the home. More gunshots sounded and I figured it was Tim. I remember him telling me about the gun he'd bought for protection a year ago at a block party. Well, the gun didn't seem to be doing much protecting now as more and more zombies filled the house. It was like there was a house party going on, only Tim and his family were the appetizers.

Tim and I had had some problems over the years, too. The one that I remember the most was when he kept parking his car in front of my house. Now, the way my street is set up is it's a one way and there is only parking on one side—on the left side. On the right side, because there's not enough parking, cars park there too but the driver's know to put their right tires on the sidewalk about two feet. That way there's room for cars to get down the street and there's also still room on the sidewalk for people to walk. But Tim, he was an asshole, and he would always put his car *three* feet on the sidewalk. I could barely get by. And then, to make matters worse, his car leaked oil. It got all over my sidewalk. I paid my taxes dammit, if anyone was going to ruin my sidewalk it should be me.

So we got into it a few times and finally, when he wouldn't stop, I put in a tree. See, the city would let you put in a tree if you wanted to pay for it. A lot of other houses on my street did this so that people wouldn't park in front of their homes. But now I lost that parking place…all thanks to Tim. And his wife Susan was no better. She was a bitch if you ask me; always turning her nose up at me when she saw me. The kids were brats, too, always playing in the street, screaming and yelling all the time.

As I watched, I saw that it wasn't going very well over at the Robbins' house. I had a pair of binoculars that I used to watch the neighborhood. Some of the wood nailed to the windows had been torn off and I could see right into the living room. Tim was on the couch with three zombies attacking him. One sank its teeth into his left cheek and then it reared back its head. Tim's cheek peeled from his face and the skin stretched like taffy, then snapped off.

The zombie shoved the flesh in its mouth and began chewing happily as blood seeped from between cracked lips. Another one scooped out Tim's left eyeball, and with the ganglia stretching like little red threads, it shoved the eyeball into its mouth. Chewing, the orb popped like a grape, spraying clear ooze back onto Tim's screaming face.

Susan was on the floor and her intestines were being pulled out, while behind her, the two kids were trapped in a corner, the zombies falling on them to tear the kids limb from limb. It looked like the kids wouldn't be coming back. There wouldn't be anything left to animate.

I lowered the binoculars and looked down at my pale hands, imagining what Tim and Susan and their kids were feeling. A chill went down my spine at the thought of it. When I looked back outside again, I could see the zombies were stepping away from

Tim and Susan, and some were going over to the kids to continue feeding. As for Susan and Tim, they were back on their feet, though worse for wear than a few minutes ago. It's amazing how fast the dead come back and I suppose that's why there are so many walkers out there.

No sooner were people killed than they would return to life, and there were almost always plenty of their bodies left to let the ghoul become mobile. The kids were small and easy to pull apart, so children usually were devoured to the point there was nothing left to reanimate.

When the two Robbins' children were nothing but bloody bones, the zombies begin to file out of the house. They were satiated, for a while anyway, but soon enough they would be on the search for more food.

There was no hiding from them; they seemed to be able to smell humans, to detect them somehow. I don't know how it worked, no one did, but what was known was that no matter where you hid, they would ferret you out sooner or later.

I spotted Sam in the crowd. He was holding some organ, a liver maybe or a kidney. Good for him, he was part of the 'in' crowd now. Even dead, I bet he was still an asshole though.

It's times like this when I wished I had a gun. I could have lined Sam's head up and blown it right off his fucking shoulders. But I don't have one. In my state in New England, gun laws are pretty strict and you kind of have to know someone to get a permit.

I don't know anyone so I never bothered trying. The city would usually turn people down who wanted a gun permit unless they had a really good reason to. I never did.

With the show over, I went back to the couch, and sat down. I was tired. I was always tired lately.

I planned to do some more writing to get it down and then I was going back to sleep.

I didn't know what time it was when the next neighbor was attacked. I saw it was night when I went to the window but that was it. It may have been that night or even days later. I'd lost all sense of time by then and sometimes I swore I slept for days before waking. I would then write some and go back to sleep. I wasn't eating anything. Nothing in the house interested me, despite the hunger in my stomach.

The neighbor on the left of me was being attacked this time. I could hear the sound of boards being ripped off windows and then the crunch of a door being kicked in.

The Simmons lived next door to me; Paul and Martha. They were an older couple in their seventies. Paul was the man's name and from the first day I met him I knew he was an asshole. He proved my point a few years later when I wanted to put up a fence on the border of my property and his. He didn't like that at all. He had a small garden he would maintain every year and when I had the land surveyed, I found out that the garden was actually on my property and that a foot of land all the way from the street to the back of the house was mine, too. The bastard had tried to claim it as his all these years. So I put up the fence without listening to his protests and he never let me forget it. He tried to sue me but I got it squashed.

Sure, I could have not put up the fence, I mean, once I had the land surveyed the one foot was mine again, as I had proof. But I put the fence up anyway, even if it pissed the old man off.

Screams of pain and anguish filled the night as the zombies entered the old couple's home and tore into them. I heard Martha screech a few times but they were mercifully short. Paul yelled out once, pleading for someone to help him and his wife. I know I wasn't going to help them. Even if there was a chance in hell I wasn't taking it. I couldn't see their house at all. It was directly on my left and I had no windows on that side on this floor. I was too weak to try and climb upstairs to my bedroom, which had a window overlooking the right side of their house, so I had to use my ears to imagine what was going on over there. I knew it probably wasn't too pretty.

Their suffering was over quickly and I never saw them again. I assumed too much of them had been eaten for them to revive. Either that or they were in pieces and the brain was still intact and they were crawling around their house, unable to leave but still one of the living dead. A chilling thought either way.

When I knew they were truly gone I went back to my couch and sat down. I grabbed a piece of paper from my stack of new ones and began to write some more. Someone needed to document all this carnage, so that when people came finally, such as the army, they could read my notes and have an idea how terrible it was for all of us.

After writing for a while I went back to sleep and didn't wake until the next morning, or perhaps it was the day after that. As I said, time held no meaning for me anymore. Other than writing my experiences, the only thing I did to pass the time was watch my neighbors when it was their time to die.

Sometime that morning—whatever day it was—my neighbors on the right side of me made a run for it, as crazy as that sounds.

Gunshots woke me as they often had in the past, and when I went to the window, I saw the Billings family that lived on the right side of me running down their cement walkway to the sidewalk, where their car was parked in front of their house. I did see that the car was a foot too close to my driveway. It wasn't the first time either, and if it wasn't for the zombies I would have probably gave Richard Billings a piece of my mind. We'd had words before about him parking too close to my driveway. I didn't use my driveway much but that didn't matter. It was the *principle* of the thing.

As soon as the couple appeared on the walkway and Richard began shooting, the zombies swarmed them. I saw it was only Richard and his wife, Mary, and for a second I wondered where their son was, but then I remembered he had joined the army. I heard he was stationed nearby but that was about it. I didn't talk to Richard much. We never stood on the sidewalk like neighbors should do, chatting about this and that or if it was going to rain later that night.

Richard was holding a handgun of some type I couldn't identify. I could see it was a pistol though. As the couple ran for their car, zombies surrounded them, wanting to make a feast of the two warm bodies. But Richard was good with his gun and he shot ghoul after ghoul, almost every bullet fired a head shot.

Then Mary screamed when a zombie grabbed her and tried to sink its teeth into her neck. Richard, acting fast, spun around and shot the zombie right between the eyes. Gore splattered outward and Mary was hit in the face with blood spatter. She screamed as the sticky stuff hit her face and Richard ran to her and pulled her from the zombie's grip, which was still holding on tight to her arm, despite being dead for good now.

"The car, the car! Get in the fucking car!" Richard screamed and shot two more zombies in the head. Mary did as she was told and opened the passenger door, then slammed the door closed once she was inside. As she closed the door, a zombie reached out for her and its fingers got caught between the door and the frame of the car. Like scissors cutting through paper, the fingers were taken off and three digits fell into Mary's lap, the digits still wiggling. Mary screamed again and franticly brushed them off her legs to the floorboard.

Richard was moving around to the back of the car, and when he was right at my driveway, I began to bang on my window between two boards to get his attention. Maybe if he saw me he would wave to me to come out and join him in escaping. But when he swiveled around to see who was banging, his eyes met mine and I saw his jaw drop. We stared at each other for a span of seconds, but to me if felt like a lifetime.

Then he turned away and got into his car as more zombies swarmed around the vehicle, banging on the hood and windows.

I stood watching, horrified and amazed at being ignored, as the car engine sputtered and then roared to life. As more zombies beat on the car, Richard put it into gear and it began to rock the car back and forth, the sheer weight of bodies preventing him from going forward. Then he got the idea to go backwards, as there weren't as many bodies near the rear bumper, most of them congregating around the steering wheel area, as that was where the two warm humans were.

The car knocked over a few bodies, then drove onto my grass, before spinning to the left and onto the street, knocking over some trashcans and spilling garbage everywhere.

Richard regained control and stopped, then put the car into drive and it jerked forward, taking down more zombies as it raced up the street.

Bodies bounced off the grille as the car swerved left and right to avoid them, but there were simply too many ghouls on the road to avoid them all. Then the car swerved around the corner at the end of the street and was gone.

They were all gone now; everyone on the street was either dead or gone.

I couldn't believe Richard had left me, especially after seeing me clear as day in the window. He'd left me to die and there was nothing I could do about it.

It doesn't matter. I don't need them anyway, bunch of selfish bastards.

People are such assholes, aren't they? They only worry about themselves all the time, no consideration for how others might feel. The only time they give you the time of day is when they need something from you.

Outside, the zombies were calming down, and other than a lot more prone bodies covering the street and sidewalk, things became quiet and stayed that way.

It would be my turn soon, I knew it. I was the last living soul on the street. Sooner or later the zombies would become hungry and they would come for me.

And there was nothing I could do to stop them.

Accepting my fate, I sat down on the couch and began writing what I'd just seen. Like I said before, someone had to do it and it made me feel good to get it all down on paper.

Time passed slowly for me then. I was the last one left on the street but for some reason the zombies didn't come for me. I would look out the window and see them standing still or walking slowly down the street aimlessly, but not once did they turn and attack my house.

More showed up as days turned into weeks but still I remained in solitude, safe but alone.

Then, one day I heard the unmistakable sound of truck engines, followed by gunshots. Excited, I went to my favorite window for watching the street and peered outside. The zombies had heard the engines and gunshots, too. They came out of houses and from backyards to gather in the street. I saw Sam there, and Karen and Tim.

Minutes passed as the gunshots grew louder, and then to my amazement and relief, a military armored personnel transport

(APC for short) turned the corner at the end of the street and began to come towards my house. It was big, with large tires. There was a soldier sticking out of the top of the vehicle and he was firing an M-60 with lethal precision. As the APC got closer, I saw zombies getting mowed down like a scythe to wheat. Bodies were stitched from groin to neck, arms and legs blown clear off torsos. Heads were hit to explode from the large bullets, brains and bone matter flying like shrapnel to pepper the other zombies.

But the dead knew no fear and they still came forward, only to be taken down one by one. The tires of the APC drove over the fallen bodies, crushing the carcasses into a red and black mush. Five zombies standing in the middle of road were run down by the APC, the corpses then mangled and turned into the consistency of soup by the already gore-covered tires. One ghoul's head was run over and it popped like a grape, the brain ejecting out of the skull cavity to slide across the ground, leaving behind it a gruesome snail trail.

It was finally over! The government was taking the world back from the dead.

I was saved!

I watched as more military vehicles arrived, some trucks with canvas covering their backs. The trucks stopped and soldiers hopped out, each one carrying an M-16 or other assault weapons. They began going from house to house, checking to see if there were any zombies inside that were too badly mangled to move, such as ones with broken legs or no feet. I heard gunshots from some of the houses as the soldiers took down any ghouls found within.

Then, finally, they came to my house. I didn't even have time to reach the front door and take down the barricade. The soldiers kicked it in, saving me the trouble. I didn't mind. I knew I would be leaving my home, probably to go to some rescue station.

Three soldiers bearing M-16s came charging through my front door, and within seconds were in my living room, the place I'd been holed up for what felt like years.

"Oh thank God you're here!" I yelled, my hands going out to embrace my saviors. "I thought I was going to die in here." I was still holding my pen, something I wanted to take with me to document my rescue.

But the soldiers didn't come to me and help me leave. Instead, all three raised their M-16s and pointed them at me.

Oh my God, what was wrong with them? Was it the bad light in the house? I was filthy from lack of bathing and my clothes weren't too clean either but surely they could see that I wasn't a walking corpse.

"No wait, what are you doing? I'm not dead, I'm alive! Don't kill me, you idiots!" I yelled.

I heard the reports a split second before the bullets hit me. Two of the men shot me in the chest, which even in my death I thought was ludicrous. After all, hadn't these men seen a zombie movie before? But one of the soldiers obviously had because his bullet struck me right between the eyes. I swear, I did feel the bullet enter my brain a split second before it went dark, then my splattered brain was decorating the wall behind me and the back of my skull was nonresistant.

My last thought was that these soldiers were truly assholes.

* * *

The three soldiers, two Privates and a Corporal, lowered their rifles and stared at the corpse before them. The body was beyond desiccated, really nothing but a skeleton with skin. In its right hand was a pen. One of the men walked over to the body and picked up one of hundreds of pieces of paper that littered the floor.

"Hey, guys, look at this."

The other two men went to the soldier to see what he'd found.

"There's all kinds of scribblings on this paper." He bent over and picked up a few more, studying them. "These have scribbles on them, too. It's like this zombie was trying to write something."

The corporal scowled. "That's impossible. The deadheads are stupid. They can't think, shithead, now cut the crap and get moving, Private. We still need to make sure the rest of this house is clear."

"You got it, Corporal," the soldier said and dropped the paper. He glanced down at the body and saw the bandage on its left arm just above the wrist. The bandage was long past being white, and was crusted with blood, pus seeping out of the edges of the wrapping. "Poor bastard," he said. "Looks like the guy got bit and then holed up in here, only to turn into one of them later."

The other private was still looking at the corpse and said, "I knew this guy."

"No shit, how so, Billings?" the corporal asked.

Private Billings shrugged. "I used to live on this street, right next door actually."

"Really? Then what about your family?"

"They were in the house I grew up in, trapped, but a few weeks ago they made a break for it and got away. They're at the rescue station out on Route 40."

"Oh, well that's good."

"Oh yeah," Private Billings replied. "I knew this guy well. He was a horror writer of some kind. He was a real asshole, too. Always arguing with everyone in the neighborhood, like he was so much better than the rest of us. He used to sit in his living room window and watch everyone with a pair of binoculars all the time. It was creepy."

The corporal merely nodded, then gestured to the doorway leading out of the room. "Come on, we've got a lot of other houses to clear before the day's over."

The two privates nodded and the three men finished checking the rest of the house, then they moved on.

VAMPIRES VS ZOMBIES

JENNIFER KOEHLER

Molly Gannon, a vampire, sat at the photo desk at *The Cincinnati Enquirer*, bored out of her mind with nothing to do. The newsroom on the nineteenth floor was quiet, except for the static of police scanners and clacking keyboards. To her right, Sam, Molly's photo editor, sat with his back to her. With a growl of frustration, he repeatedly pounded on his keyboard trying so that his computer would finally comply.

Molly sighed as she stretched and ran her fingers through her long, dark curly hair. It was a slow news day. She listened to Sam's heartbeat. It was music to her vampire ears. His blood soared through his veins, rising to a crescendo as his blood pressure crept to a dangerous level. Molly opened her ears and listened to the heartbeat of every human in the building, a beautiful symphony that sent shivers of lust along her spine. She arched her back and opened her mouth with a gasp. Her sharp fangs slowly eased their way out of her gums; she was ready to feed.

Their blood was seductive.

Molly sighed again as her fangs receded into her gums. An unoccupied vampire is a dangerous vampire.

She closed her hearing to the rhythmic, delicious pattern that seemed to pulse against the inside of her own ribcage. To distract herself, she gazed out of the wide windows that looked eastward. Cincinnati's *skyscrapers*—the PNC building, Carew Tower, the Scripps building—reached for the white, puffy clouds above. The clouds raced across the blue sky, chasing the wind around the Queen City. The polluted, mud-brown Ohio River raged with choppy, lashing waves while trash floated neatly across its surface.

Despite well-known vampire lore, the sun didn't turn vampires into a pile of ash or encase them in a crispy outer crust. Vampires walked around in the sunlight like any normal human. There was simple mythology created by vampires to keep the human population unaware of their existence, allowing Molly to walk as a predator among the human cattle.

Molly's fascination with the clouds and river broke when a dispatcher called out over the police scanner.

"White male in his 30s, wearing jeans and yellow hoodie, collapsed on the Purple People Bridge. Witnesses say he's not breathing."

Anxious to get away from her coworkers, Molly grabbed her gear and left Sam to curse at his computer. She ran at her top vampire speed through the building and the city streets, a blur at the edge of human perception. Within seconds, she arrived at the scene. Running with her preternatural speed always pleased her; she was like Superman, running faster than a speeding train, one hundred times faster. She could wave to a smiling boy looking out a passenger car window, but he would never see her, his human eye too slow to perceive her presence. Her speed allowed her a professional advantage. Always the first on the scene, her photos were taken, transmitted, and posted to the newspaper's website before TV crews could set up their cameras.

At the bridge, a small group of people stood around gawking as a Good Samaritan administered CPR to the collapsed man, who lay sprawled in a yellow, stained hoodie. Molly couldn't hear a heartbeat. His open, bloodshot eyes were lifeless. She knew that look all too well. He was already gone, but the would-be savior kept pumping his chest.

Sirens wailed in the distance, a stark contrast against the calm day's bright, hopeful sky.

Molly continued working the scene, taking pictures of by-standers, the Good Samaritan, and the collapsed man. As she worked, the witnesses shared their experiences with each other.

"Yeah, man, he was staggerin' across the bridge from the Kentucky side. I thought he was drunk, but when he fell and didn't get back up—man I knew something was wrong."

"Oh, man, he's dead. His skin's all pale and gray."

"Anyone know what happened to him?" Molly asked. "Know what made him collapse?"

The witnesses looked at each other and shrugged.

"What was he doing right before he fell?" Molly asked.

Again they looked at each other. "Well," one said. "He was coughing something fierce."

"And shivering," another said.

Molly studied the corpse. Armpit stains darkened the yellow hoodie to a deep shade of ochre. Molly's sensitive, enhanced sense of smell was assaulted by the light breeze, which carried a subtle hint of rotten meat entangled with the scent of musty sweat and Axe body wash. Tears sprang to her eyes as she choked back a gag. He smelled as if he'd been dead for a very long time. For a human, the dead man radiated a foul odor unlike any Molly had the misfortune of inhaling.

The sirens cut off as the ambulance and police arrived. Quickly, they began to work. The police and the paramedics pushed aside the Good Samaritans and the rumbling crowd. Through her lens, Molly captured it all. The paramedics tried to pull the man's life out of the ether with their life-saving procedures, but it was clear the man was dead. Once they called it, they put their equipment away and began wrapping the body for transportation.

As police officers interviewed the witnesses, Molly lingered in the crowd, firing off shots. Amidst the commotion, a faint sound caught Molly's attention—a gurgling sound followed by a short and shallow intake of breath. She watched the paramedics as they stuffed the dead man into a body bag. And again, in between the crinkles of plastic, she heard it.

Gurgle. Inhale. Crinkle. Gurgle. Crinkle. Inhale. Moan.

Interested in the breathing corpse, Molly walked over to the paramedics, who didn't seem to notice that their recently deceased patient was breathing. She unzipped the bag and stared into the corpse's blank, dead eyes. Molly still couldn't hear a heartbeat, but there was no mistaking the breathing.

Molly switched her camera from photos to video.

Once again the dead body moaned, and she pressed the shutter to begin recording. This time one of the paramedics heard it and jumped back.

"What the hell, Carl?" the other paramedic yelled.

"He's breathing."

"What? No, he's not."

"Dude, he just moaned."

"Carl, we've had this discussion. Dead bodies sometimes make noises as they expel gas."

"Dan," Carl pointed a shaking finger, "he's *looking* at you!"

Molly focused the camera on the dead man's face; his eyes—milky white with a hint of brown—were still lifeless, but somehow aware.

They blinked.

Dan screamed a high-pitched, little girl scream and jumped as far back as his large body would allow.

The few witnesses who remained gasped collectively. The air was still and quiet as the dead man blinked and moaned again. Everyone stood frozen in place, trying to wrap their brains around what they were seeing, Molly included. This wasn't the sort of undead she knew about. This was something else.

She continued to record the event.

Again the dead body moaned. Louder. Longer. It inhaled and moaned again—louder and even longer than before.

The dead man in the yellow hoodie screamed an agonized and tormented scream.

Then the screaming stopped and hung in the air like a low dense fog. After a few beats of silence the dead man sat up. He sniffed the air and slowly turned towards Dan. He grunted as he freed himself from the plastic body bag.

Grunt. Crinkle. Grunt.

With its vacant eyes trained on Dan, the corpse in the stained, yellow hoodie let out a final, guttural roar and launched at the paramedic. Frozen in a state of shock, Dan didn't move, and the dead man sank his teeth deep into the large paramedic's meaty neck.

The sound of tearing flesh and muscle made Molly want to vomit, but the smell of blood was too appetizing. Molly bit back her own supernatural hunger to finish taping the scene as it played out. She knew it was heartless; there was no helping poor Dan, and she knew this video would get a *ton* of hits on the website.

As Dan fell to the ground with the dead man on top, panic spread like wildfire through the remaining eyewitnesses. They screamed and ran in every direction. One person jumped over the side of the bridge. The cops tried to keep order, but it was useless. They attempted to pull the dead man off Dan, but the hungry corpse thrashed and bit one of the policemen, drawing more blood and screams. The other cops brandished their guns and riddled the corpse with round after round until their clips were empty.

When the smoke cleared, both Dan and the dead man were on the ground, their heads a mess of gore and brain fragments. The three blood-spattered policemen frantically reloaded their weapons and once again leveled them at two bodies, shouting at one another while they worked. Why was Dan also headless? In the fog of battle, Molly was sure they'd fired on him, too.

"Fucker bit me," one of the panting officers looked over his wounded forearm.

The crowd had dissipated and only the three cops, Carl the paramedic, and Molly the photojournalist were left standing in a state of silent shock. The silence only lasted a few minutes until one of the cops noticed Molly's camera. She stopped recording as the wounded officer approached with a half crazed, half bewildered look on his face.

"Molly, isn't it? We've seen you around before. You can't be here. Give me your camera."

Molly pulled the camera out of his reach. "Uh, no."

The cop reached for the camera with his bloodied hand. Molly caught his wrist in mid-air and applied enough pressure to let him know she could pulverize every bone if she so chose. The scent of his blood tickled her vampire senses. Instead of smelling mouthwateringly delicious, it smelled of rot.

"Don't do that," she insisted. "I have every right to be here."

He whimpered in pain. "You can't release this. There will be panic."

She squeezed him a bit harder and shoved the arm in his face.

"You see this?" His wound stopped bleeding and started oozing a black pus-like substance. His blood reeked of decay and death. She wouldn't drink it if he were the last human on Earth. The veins in his arm turned black with the infection. "You have a hell of a lot more to worry about then any information *The Enquirer* puts out. People need to know what's coming for them."

His green eyes grew wide with fear as he studied his wound. She released him, and he ran back to the remaining paramedic.

Molly walked away from the scene at a human's pace and once she was clear of prying eyes, ran as fast as she could back to the

Enquirer building on Elm. When she returned to her office, she quickly downloaded the video and played it for Sam, who was willing to stop long enough from his labors at the computer to share her horrendous experience.

"This isn't real," he said. "This can't be real."

"It's real," Molly replied.

"I don't understand what I'm seeing."

"It's simple, Sam. He was dead. Then he wasn't. Then he ate the paramedic. The cops killed him. Now he's really dead. Head blown to bits. Do you think we should put this on the website?"

Without saying a word, Sam bolted from his chair and in the direction of the men's room.

Yellow and tangerine flames streaked across the cerulean sky as the setting sun disappeared below the horizon, the flaming yellow ball of fire conceding to the cold blackness of night. Her shift over, Molly left the Enquirer building and stepped into the twilight. The streets of Cincinnati bustled with rush hour traffic as people made their mass exodus out of downtown anxious to put the day's work behind them.

Eager to have a drink with her boyfriend Trent, Molly walked in the direction of Fountain Square. A cool breeze ruffled her long, black hair as she walked down the alley between the Enquirer building and the backside of the business facing Fourth Street. The flowery scent of her shampoo swirled into the air as she opened her ears to the city around her. She ignored the thumping car radios, blaring horns, and intermittent petty arguments. Instead, Molly kept her ears tuned in for the unusual. The moaning of the dead man in the yellow hoodie plagued her thoughts as she walked. She left her coworkers in stunned silence as they watched and re-watched her video, their lives forever changed. Mildly disturbed by the man in the yellow hoodie, Molly couldn't shake the feeling that by the end of the night, her life would be forever changed.

Ruminating, she walked along the deserted and dark alley, the security lights broken or burned out. Not that it mattered much to Molly—her vampire eyes didn't need much light to pierce the dark. She walked slowly, enjoying the echoing sound of her boots on the brick and concrete buildings around her. Above, somewhere tied to a fire escape, wind chimes sang a soft, eerie tone. Then, between footsteps, a rustling sound whispered in the darkness. She turned and noticed nothing.

Must have been a piece of paper in the breeze, Molly assured herself.

She continued on her way until she heard the rustling again, followed by a slow, agonizing groan. Molly stopped and listened with her vampire ears.

Once again, she was immediately reminded of the corpse on the bridge.

The moan returned, a little louder this time. Molly turned and saw something crawl from beneath a dumpster. The figure crawled slowly on hands and knees while moaning a sad, pathetic moan. Intrigued, Molly watched as the figure rose to its feet and stood in the middle of the alley.

The crawler was a young girl who stood motionless fifty or so feet away in that dark alley. Her jeans, worn Superman t-shirt, and tattered white tennis shoes were covered in dirt and dead human blood. Her straight blonde hair, crusted with blood and torn flesh, hung past her shoulders. A gaping wound in her left bicep oozed black pus. Slowly, it ran the length of her arm and down to her fingertips. Every few seconds, a drop fell to the concrete. Drip. Black, spider-veins sprouted from the wound.

Drip. The veins ran up the girl's neck. Drip. They covered the left side of her face like tree branches. Drip.

Molly studied the girl's milky blue eyes—devoid of life, but still seeing. If Molly could feel hot or cold she would have shivered.

Again, the girl moaned.

She listened for the girl's heartbeat, the flow of blood through her veins. Molly heard nothing but silence from her heart. This girl was dead.

Again, the girl moaned, even louder, as she stretched out a dead hand toward Molly and took a step forward.

"Little girl, what happened to you?" Molly asked.

The girl cocked her head to the side, moaned—still louder—and took another step forward.

The scent of the girl rode the tail-end of the wind and slammed into Molly's hyper-sensitive vampire olfactory senses like a sledgehammer. Never had Molly smelled something so foul and rotten. Since being turned into a vampire, she'd smelled some pretty awful things. This little girl smelled worse than putrid flesh-she was death personified.

Another breeze and this time, the girl caught Molly's scent. She lifted her nose to the air, inhaled, and took another step forward. One step. Two. On the third step, the creature sprinted toward Molly, a feral growl escaping from its dead lips. Molly stood her ground; she wasn't intimidated by a young girl.

When she was close enough, the girl launched herself at Molly. The girl's stench embraced Molly as she grabbed a hold of her shoulders and wrapped her legs around Molly's waist. Ripping through the fabric of Molly's jacket and t-shirt, the girl's fingers dug deeply into Molly's flesh like five dull knives. To Molly's surprise, she could smell her own blood-vampire blood had a distinctive scent all its own.

"Ow! You little..." Molly tried to pull the girl off of her. Molly wouldn't be able to feel pain unless it was inflicted upon her by another vampire, and that girl wasn't a vampire, yet, the pain was real.

What are you? Molly wondered.

Molly grabbed the girl by the hair just as her teeth grazed Molly's neck. Molly pulled with all of her supernatural strength and only managed to scalp the girl. The skin slipped off the top of the girl's skull like a bean pops out of its shell, the sound of tearing flesh barely audible over the girl's growl. Undeterred by pain, the girl gnashed her teeth at Molly with renewed vigor.

Molly quickly dropped the girl's scalp to the ground—it landed with a squishy splash—and grabbed her by the neck. Eye to milky, dead eye, with her attacker, Molly noticed small chunks of flesh in the girl's teeth as she pulled her cracked lips back in a fearsome snarl. Her teeth snapped at Molly, anxious to get a bite in. Molly gagged, and the blood she had for lunch slithered into the back of her throat.

The girl's fingers dug deeper into Molly's shoulders, tearing the flesh. Not giving into the pain caused by this wretched girl, Molly tightened her vice like grip on the girl's throat. The flesh, soft and mushy in Molly's hand, began to tear. The girl only struggled harder, dug her fingers deeper, and tore a chunk of skin from Molly's right shoulder.

Molly refused to scream and channeled her pain into ripping the girl's head from her shoulders. Molly already survived one brutal attack in an alley—she wasn't about to be taken down by some dead little girl. She put all of her vampire strength and rage into squeezing the girl's throat until her spine was severed. Her head popped off like a Barbie doll's, minus the hollow plastic pop—skin tore, muscles snapped, and Molly's hands were left moist and wet with decaying blood. The girl's body went limp, released Molly from her grasp, and fell to the ground with a satisfying thud.

The head, on the other hand, continued to silently chomp its teeth at Molly.

Molly threw the head to the ground and crushed it beneath the heel of her boot until nothing but a globulous mass of blood, cartilage, and bone was left. Her own enhanced strength allowed her the niceties of glorifying in such a hard-earned victory.

Again, the breeze blew through the alley. High above the wind, chimes continued their eerie tune, and the realization that she just killed a young girl sunk in. Vampires had but one rule—no children. Never, under any circumstances, are vampires to harm a child. To do so would mean severe punishment and death.

"I'm so sorry," Molly whispered.

She pulled out her cell phone and texted the cleanup crew for help. "Incident. Request services. Benham Alley beside Enquirer building."

Tom's text-reply read: "U got it beautiful."

Within minutes, identical twins Tom and Jerry pulled up in an unmarked white van. Molly was pleasantly surprised; the side door slid open and her boyfriend Trent jumped off the van and was at her side before it came screeching to a halt.

"Baby," she said. "You didn't need to be here. I can handle it."

Trent was the unofficial leader of the "Cincinnati Crew" of vampires. When he arrived in Cincinnati, Trent naturally fell into the role. Back in his human years, he'd been boss of an Irish gang called "The Gougers" in Chicago. Leadership fit him like a fine Italian leather jacket. Molly had loved him since she was human. She'd fallen in love with his long, lustrous black curly hair, ocean blue eyes, and deep, sultry voice.

"I have no doubt," he said, his face twisted with worry. Trent noticed her bloodied shoulder, and shock mingled with his worry. The wound already began to heal, but Molly would need to feed soon in order for it to heal completely.

"Don't worry," Molly said as she embraced him. "I'm okay."

"Did a vampire do this?" Trent clenched his shaking fists; rage was ready to be unleashed.

Molly shook her head.

Tom came around the other side of the van. "What the hell happened here?" He then spotted the dead girl. "Molly, this is a kid."

"Take a deep breath, Tom," Molly replied. "She's not human. Or at least she wasn't when she attacked me."

"Man! That's disgusting," Tom declared.

Jerry, his often-silent identical twin brother, tossed Tom a blue body bag from the back of the van.

The twins were the brothers Molly never had. Tom, loud and boisterous, was all talk and bravado. Jerry was more reserved, but carried himself with quiet confidence. Both were the most brutal members of the Cincinnati crew. Other vampires fled in terror at the very mention of their names. But to Molly, they were the protective and sometimes overbearing big brothers.

"How could she not be human?" Trent walked over to inspect the girl.

Tom began unfolding the body bag, the sound of the crinkling plastic echoing off the brick buildings, a valley of darkness in the otherwise bright city with its evening streets awash in electric light.

"I swear she didn't have a heartbeat, but she still attacked me," Molly said. "This girl wasn't a vampire. Vampires don't smell like that. And they certainly don't try to *eat* other vampires."

"*Eat!*" the three of them said in unison.

"Yes, eat," Molly replied. "Look at my shoulder."

Tom and Jerry came over to inspect Molly's battle wound. "She didn't actually bite you, did she?" Tom asked.

Molly replayed the fight in her head before answering. "No, but she came close."

"Good," Tom then returned to his brother. "We don't know what a zombie bite will do to a vampire."

"Zombie, huh," Molly recalled the dead man in the yellow hoodie. Zombie seemed an apt description. She wondered how many more roamed the city.

"Zombie." Trent scoffed. "How do you know what a zombie is, Tom?"

"You know, like in *Night of the Living Dead*?" He stuck his arms straight out in front of him. "Braaaiinnns!"

"I read books," Trent said. "I don't waste my time with television."

"Oh right, because you're old," Tom snickered. "They didn't have TV when you were fangless."

Trent rolled his eyes at Tom and returned his attention to Molly.

"I'm okay," she said. "I promise."

The twins worked methodically and quickly, wiping all traces of the fight in the alley. Most of their calls were from unruly vampires who grew greedy or killed an innocent. All jobs were rushed, and there was no room for error. Within minutes, the girl's body was loaded in the van; the alley was cleaned of gelatinous goo and the air treated to mask the coppery scent of blood from other predators. Except for the gaping wound in Molly's right shoulder, it was almost like the fight had never happened. Before Molly could thank them for their efforts, Tom's cell phone buzzed.

"Got another incident," Tom said as he checked his phone. "The vampires are misbehavin' tonight."

"Go take care of it," Trent replied. "I'll get Molly to the Grotto."

"See ya," Tom said as he jumped into the driver's seat. Jerry only nodded as he followed his brother's lead and got into the van. The van rumbled to life, then disappeared into the night. Molly and Trent were left standing in the darkened alley to contemplate the dead girl in the blue body bag.

"She was strong, Trent," Molly said. "I could barely tear her off me."

She studied her blood stained hands. The smell of the girl's rotten blood lingered on Molly's skin. She frantically wiped her hands on her jeans to get the stench off.

"Let's get you to the Grotto," Trent said as he took Molly by the hand. "You need to feed."

The cold black of night banished the yellow-orange fire of the sun from the cerulean sky. In Fountain Square, a local band played their rendition of "Smooth" by Carlos Santana and Rob Thomas. The music bounced off the high-rise buildings surrounding the square as a group of young professionals swayed to the music in front of the stage. Instead of an uproar of applause, the end of the song was greeted with screams of terror and agonizing pain.

The coppery scent of fresh blood filled the air, as limbs were plucked from bodies like petals from a flower. Zombies cared not for the "he loves me, he loves me not" scenario. It was meat they were after, and the young professionals celebrating the end of a workday offered them a feast, and so the dead ate.

The fresh blood in the air beckoned to Molly like a seductive temptress. She and Trent rushed to the square, where the stench of decay overpowered the luscious aroma of human blood.

The Genius of Water stood at the top of the famous Tyler Davidson Fountain, her arms outstretched—open and inviting—as she bestowed the gift of water from her hands. From her lofty perch, the water rained down with a slightly tinted red hue as zombie-eaten bodies floated in the fountain's pools.

Bodies were torn limb from limb, overturned tables, chairs, and table umbrellas littered the Square. Discarded cell phones, purses, wallets, and unfinished alcoholic drinks were left behind. Musical instruments were left abandoned on the stage where nameless local bands usually played.

In front of the stage, where a horde of drunk and dancing young professionals should have been, a small group of zombies greedily feasted on a woman. Hands deep in the woman's entrails and her blood dripping from their lips, the group didn't notice Molly and Trent as they approached. Not wanting to alert them to their presence, the vampires spoke to each other telepathically.

What do we do? Do we stop them? Molly asked her lover.

No Molly, the woman is already dead.

Need I remind you, lover, that one of these things hurt me?

Molly pointed to her wounded shoulder, and anger contorted Trent's face.

You said they were strong.

Yes, but they don't have our speed. And their heads pop off pretty easily.

Trent nodded.

Go for the head, Trent. Decapitate and stomp it to mush.

In a flash, Molly and Trent had a decapitated head in each hand. They threw the heads down and ground them into the stone pavers with the heels of their boots.

Only one remained.

A man, dressed in a business suit with a loosened tie around his neck. A gaping wound on his shoulder wept thick black pus as black, spidery veins slithered up the side of his neck. He continued to feast on the dead woman and didn't seem to notice that dining companions were missing.

Trent clucked at the zombie to get his attention. The corpse snapped his head up, an unidentifiable organ between his teeth, and focused on Trent. The zombie spit out the organ and rose from his meal, ready for fresh meat.

"Be careful, Trent," Molly said.

"Come here, boy," Trent said. "Come meet your true death."

The zombie businessman growled as he staggered toward Trent. The vampire easily caught him by the throat, lifted him from his feet, and body-slammed him into the ground. Molly heard the crack of bones as the businessman smashed into the stone pavers. He continued to snarl at Trent as his fingers clawed at flesh, ripping and tearing, trying to eat. Trent lifted him from the ground, revealing the cracked stone pavers underneath, and slammed him down again. This time, the businessman's head cracked open and his body went limp. His mouth, however, still moved with gnashing teeth. Trent kicked him repeatedly in the head until the teeth were nothing but dust.

"Feel better?" Molly asked.

Trent looked up at her with a malevolence she'd never seen from him. Molly knew exactly who and what her boyfriend was, but for the first time, she truly saw the monster within. She'd seen him kill before, but never with such hatred.

She pulled him away from the bloody mess at his feet, smoothed back hair that had fallen into his eyes, and forced him to look at her. Contempt and fury filled his lustrous, ocean-blue eyes. Molly held his head in her hands as she rested her forehead against his. She thought of the first day they met and projected the memory towards Trent. Together and telepathically, they shared the moment they first met. An inexplicable moment where she fell in love with him and knew her life would be forever intertwined with his. After a few minutes, the softness and kindness Molly knew crept back into those ocean blue eyes. Trent kissed and embraced Molly.

"We need to go," he said.

"Cleanup crew?" Molly asked.

Trent pulled out his cell phone and sent a text. Without waiting for the twins to arrive, they continued to make their way toward the Grotto. They walked to the northwest corner of the Square to the elevators which led to the parking garage. They took the stairs. Quickly, they reached the fourth floor. When Fountain Square was renovated and the garage built, Trent made sure the architects, foremen, and most of the workers were vampires. They conveniently built a secret entrance to the Grotto.

On the fourth floor, hidden in the far southeast corner and to the left of the Fifth Street exit, was a concrete door. There was nothing spectacular about the door; it was just a door without a handle. All one had to do to open it was simply push. Vampires operated the garage, so there was no chance of human discovery. To the human eye, the door looked like nothing more than cracks in the concrete. Even if humans did see the door and tried to open it, they would need the help of heavy machinery or vampiric strength—the door was eight feet thick.

The path to that door in the far southeast corner was littered with zombies. Molly stared at them in disbelief. It was only a few hours ago that she encountered her first zombie on the Purple People Bridge, and now every small pocket of the city seemed to be crawling with them. Their moans reverberated off the concrete walls as they shuffled aimlessly back and forth—limbs half rotted or torn off—covered in dried blood and filth. Some zombies stumbled around naked, their bodies covered in the deepest of black spider veins and purple bruises—their skin torn and oozing black pus.

Molly finally wondered where all of the police were, or the National Guard. What was happening to their city?

"What's going on here?" Molly asked. "How do these things exist?"

"Don't know," Trent shrugged. "We exist, so why can't they?"

The elevator at the far end of the garage chimed, signaling its arrival. In unison, the zombies' moans increased with volume and urgency. They swarmed the elevator as screams from the occupants within pierced through the moans. Within seconds, the screams stopped, and all Molly could hear with her vampire ears was grunting zombies as their gnashing teeth ripped flesh and scraped against bone.

Intent on the beasts on the far side of the garage, Trent and Molly didn't notice the couple behind them until the woman screamed, drawing the attention of the zombies. One by one their heads snapped up, their lifeless eager eyes gazing upon them with insatiable lust.

The woman continued to scream. Her partner tried to silence her, but his attempt at soothing coos only seemed to upset her more. Her mind continued to crack, as the grunts and moans of the zombies grew louder. En masse, the zombies moved in their direction. If Molly didn't know better, she would think they were in Michael Jackson's "Thriller" video.

Trent chuckled at Molly's thought. "I think it's time to leave."

Molly nodded, turned, and grabbed the screaming woman by the arm as Trent took her partner. The couple allowed Molly and Trent to lead them up the stairs. Trent paused long enough to pull the doors to the stairwell shut.

"But our car," the man said as they ran up the stairs.

"Don't worry," Trent replied. "Zombies probably can't drive."

They reached the top floor; Molly and Trent were back where they started. Molly's shoulder continued to ache, and the blood of the two human strangers piqued her appetite. The couple's terrified heartbeats did nothing but aggravate her hunger. Her vampire-infected blood screamed through her veins, begging her to take one little sip. Humans were oh-so-delectable when they were afraid.

Molly pushed her supernatural hunger aside. She didn't feed on the innocent.

They stood in the elevator enclosure, the woman nearly hyperventilating, the man bewildered and dumbfounded as he paced. She clasped a necklace in her hands as she prayed between frantic breaths. Molly took the petite strawberry blonde by the shoulders; her hazel eyes refused to look at Molly as they darted back and forth.

"It's okay," Molly said. "You're going to be okay." Vampires had a hypnotic affect on humans. Their voices were soft and melodic to the human ear, their faces seemingly angelic. It was all part of the vampire infection that raged through their veins—vampire characteristics designed to lure their prey.

After a few attempts at placation, the woman's terrified heartbeats calmed. She stopped praying and released her necklace to reveal a simple golden crucifix.

"What's your name?" Molly asked as she wiped the tears from the woman's cheeks.

"Anne," she replied.

"I'm Molly."

"Nice to meet you," Anne said.

Anne's partner continued to pace the length of the elevator enclosure, nervously running his hands through his own thick, blonde hair.

"Now Anne," Molly said. "Do you know what those monsters are?"

She shook her head no.

"They're zombies."

Disbelief claimed Anne's face.

"It's true," Molly replied. "Now you can either deny or accept it. If you want to survive this you have to keep control of yourself. Do you understand?"

"Yes," she whispered.

"Can I count on you to keep control of yourself?" Molly asked.

"Yes."

"Good. I don't want to hear another scream from your lips unless you're being attacked. Got it?"

Anne nodded.

"That goes for you, too..."

"Darren," Anne's partner said as he stopped pacing. He took Anne into his arms and gave her a reassuring kiss on the forehead.

Molly said, "Darren, nice to meet you. You okay here?"

"Yes."

"Molly," Trent said. "We have a problem." He looked through the windows and out onto the Square. Zombies flooded the area. They moved quickly with intent, their dead eyes locked onto their next meal, and that's when Molly noticed Tom and Jerry, the apples of the zombies' eyes. Eternally hungry, they raced forward, eager to sink their teeth into the twins. Molly felt their terror rise as the zombies approached, but ever the proud vampires, they were only slightly terrified as they stood their ground.

The first zombie reached Tom, a young heavy-set woman freshly turned. Dressed for a night out with the girls in a low-cut, slimming black blouse, jeans, and calf-high black leather boots. Her prominently displayed heavy cleavage, expertly styled bouffant, and perfectly applied makeup, made her a pretty zombie. If it weren't for the growling and the bite wound on her forearm bleeding black pus, one would think she was just a normal girl. Before she could have her first taste of vampire flesh, Tom promptly decapitated her with his bare hands and stomped her brains to bits. Molly could hear the bones crack from across the Square. Both Anne and Darren gasped.

Within seconds, another zombie attacked Tom, while Jerry fended off his own zombie admirer. Trent rushed to the aid of his friends.

"Whatever you do," Molly said to Anne and Darren. "Do not leave this building."

Molly, more than slightly terrified, followed Trent into the throngs of the ravenous undead.

Trent rushed onto Fountain Square, clearing a path to the twins. With lightning-fast speed, he removed zombie heads from zombie bodies and tossed them aside to be dealt with later. But as soon as one zombie fell to the ground headless, there was another stumbling over its immobilized comrade, relentlessly charging for one tiny taste of flesh.

Molly followed close behind, decapitating, dismembering, and eviscerating as many zombies as she could.

Still, they kept coming.

Covered in stagnant blood and black pus, they reached Tom and Jerry on the "dance floor" by the stage. Within seconds, a wall of clawing, undead fingers enclosed the four of them. Zombie arms reached and struggled to get closer, as the moans grew louder and louder. Molly's ears and brains reverberated with the sound. She was overwhelmed with the urge to moan as well.

Instead she screamed, a loud, piercing scream of rage.

It may have felt good for Molly to scream and relieve her stress while she ripped apart yet another zombie, but her scream only excited the undead more. They attacked with renewed vitality.

Closer and closer, the zombies came. The four vampires had been forced to fight with their backs pressed together. Then it happened.

A terrified scream to Molly's right.

"The bastard bit me!" Tom shrieked as he tore the head off the offending zombie.

"You okay?" Molly asked.

"Fine, don't worry about me."

They continued to fight until the moans grew silent, and the throng of zombies was lying dead at their feet, decapitated heads sufficiently stomped to mush. The last two zombies destroyed, sadly, were Anne and Darren.

Again Tom screamed, this time an agonizing, painful scream.

Jerry rushed to his brother's side. Tom roughly shoved him aside, and Jerry flew backwards, landing in the zombie-polluted Tyler Davidson Fountain.

Tom fell to the ground and writhed in pain, until he abruptly became still.

Fifty feet away, Molly listened for his heartbeat. It still raged in his chest as blood coursed through his veins. Jerry pulled himself from the infested water. Dripping, he stood by the fountain and kept the distance between himself and his brother.

Tom stirred.

Jerry dripped.

Molly and Trent exchanged a look from across the Square.

Tom stood, and Molly saw the bite mark on his hand. Black pus dripped from the wound as the tell-tale veins crawled up his forearm to the bicep which disappeared beneath the sleeve of his t-shirt; the veins reappeared on his neck and face, framing his eyes like a Mike Tyson tattoo.

Torment and anguish filled his once kind, soulful brown eyes. Molly read his thoughts.

Hungry. So hungry. Meat, need meat. No, don't want this. Molly looks tasty.

In an instant, Tom locked eyes with Molly and closed the fifty-foot distance. Molly crashed to the ground with Tom, fangs and teeth gnashing, on top of her. His breath, rotten and foul, caressed her cheek.

Molly dug her fingers into Tom's throat. She twisted and pulled until a meaty chuck fell into her hand. Tom, undeterred, continued to bite at her. His teeth grazed her chin when Trent appeared and grabbed Tom by the hair; Trent tossed him across the Square. He landed in the middle of Fifth Street.

Without missing a beat, Tom was on his feet and charging at Molly again.

"I got this, babe," Molly said to Trent as she quickly got to her feet.

She braced herself for a fight as Tom raced toward her with all his vampire strength and gnashing teeth. She sidestepped, grabbed him by the arm, and hurled him to the stone pavers and pinned both arms behind his back. Molly placed a knee in the small of his back for good measure.

"Jerry," Trent said. "Would you be so kind to get Tom some restraints?"

Without a word, Jerry ran to the cleanup van parked on Vine Street. Tom struggled against Molly's grasp.

She again read his thoughts.

Hungry so hungry. Just a bite. One bite. Please.

"Tom," Trent said. "Calm down."

Tom fought harder against Molly's grasp. Molly could hold her own, even against the old vampires. But Tom's newfound cravings, added to his need for blood, seemed to be stronger, making him more dangerous. Weakened by the gaping hole in her shoulder and her own unsatisfied hunger, Molly lost her grip on Tom.

Within seconds, he had Molly pinned and his teeth were in her flesh.

Molly screamed, the burning pain was nearly unbearable.

Trent ripped Tom away from Molly, and a chunk of flesh from her neck and left shoulder went with him. He chomped and swallowed, the morsel falling out of the gaping hole in his throat.

Jerry returned with a braided rope of vampire hair and an ashwood stake stained with vampire blood.

Trent grabbed the ash wood stake from Jerry and shoved it as hard as he could into Tom's brain. Immobilized, Tom collapsed to the ground. Jerry handed the braided rope to Trent, picked up his brother, and carried him to the van.

Molly felt the zombie infection fight to gain control of her vampire blood. Equally strong, neither infection won the war; instead, Molly simply became infected with another supernatural disease.

Then it hit her like a car smashing into a concrete wall at one hundred miles an hour.

The hunger.

It's no wonder the zombies screamed when they reanimated. This hunger didn't even compare to a vampire's bloodlust, although that craving was still there. The two cravings mingled with each other. Blood, flesh, meat; Molly wanted it all. The fresher the better.

Molly shrieked like a wounded banshee.

Trent took her in his arms and carried her to the van. As soon as he shut the doors, Jerry floored it.

"You need to restrain me," Molly groaned.

Trent kissed her softly on the forehead. "No."

The van squealed into the Fifth Street Garage and smashed through the barriers. A couple of zombies stood in the path of the van. Jerry didn't let up as he drove right over them.

"If you don't," Molly said, fighting the hunger, "I'll bite you."

"No."

On the third floor, a Smart Car blocked the path of the van. Inside was a zombie, strapped in by the seatbelt, too stupid to free itself.

Jerry plowed the van into the Smart Car and pushed it into the concrete wall of the garage. He quickly reversed the van and continued to the fourth floor, where the crowd of zombies Trent and Molly encountered earlier still blocked the entrance to the Grotto. Without hesitation, Jerry plowed through them, taking down at least ten.

"*Do it now!*" she roared and lunged at him, her teeth grazing his cheek before Trent pushed her back. The van rocked with the force of their struggle.

Jerry whipped the van around the curve, pulled forward, and then backed the van up to the concrete door that led to their safe haven. He left enough room for the back doors to open.

Trent took the braided rope and quickly tied Molly's hands and feet.

"Thank you," she said. "Now gag me."

"Molly, no," Trent said. Pain emanated from his deep blue eyes, and Molly could only think of how they would taste after gouging them out with her fingers.

Jerry shut off the van, and then crawled into the back, over Molly, Trent, and his staked brother. He opened the back doors as the remaining zombies rushed the van. The van rocked as dead hands pounded on metal.

"Better do it, Trent," Jerry said as he pushed the concrete door open. He dragged his brother out of the van and slung him over his shoulder. "We don't have time to waste."

Without a word, Trent placed another braided rope into Molly's mouth and tied it at the base of her skull.

Tighter.

He obliged.

Trent picked up the love of his eternal life and carried her through the entrance to the Grotto. The thick door swung shut behind them, and with vampire speed, their loved ones over their shoulders, Trent and Jerry raced deep beneath the streets of Cincinnati to the underground vampire city.

Their bodies cut the air like a surgical blade through flesh as they ran. The breeze created in their wake blew out the candles in the three-tiered, cast iron chandeliers above, leaving darkness behind. The path ahead, lit with soft yellow light, was warm and inviting.

Soft cones of light clung to the base of the chandeliers and stretched below, creating a perfect circle on the concrete floor. Between those cones of light, on each side of the concrete tunnel, torches hung on the walls. Tongues of fire flickered, creating and destroying shadows as they licked and devoured the oxygen in the air.

Underneath Walnut Street, the vampires ran. The usual rumble of traffic above: thumping music, blaring car horns, was missing tonight. The street above was silent as the blood inside Molly's veins raged. She swallowed another scream that was building in her throat. Trent squeezed her into his chest in an attempt at comfort.

"It's going to be okay," he whispered.

I'm so hungry. You smell so...tasty....succulent. Please, just one little bite, Trent. Just one.

Molly chewed at the gag in her mouth, a desperate attempt to free herself. Her struggle was futile. Frustrated, her bones aching and the terrible hunger within burning, she screamed against her gag.

They took a left at Court Street, a right below Race Street, and entered the Grotto at the main entrance at Race and Central Parkway. The Grotto, built under the guise of a subway system back in the 1920s, still resembled a subway. The underground vampire city housed an inbound and outbound tunnel with a large platform between. The Grotto was two city blocks wide and seven city blocks long from Plum Street to Sycamore Street, with direct access to the Hamilton County Justice Center and Jail. Massive concrete pillars placed in strategic areas on the platform held up the twenty-five foot ceilings. Tapestries, elaborately embroidered, hung between the square pillars, creating makeshift rooms for vampires and their guests. From the ceiling hung giant, cast iron chandeliers, creating the intimate atmosphere vampires craved.

Each tunnel held several bars, tables, chairs, and hot tubs with cascading waterfalls. The walls on either side of the cavernous room were decorated from floor to ceiling with Rookwood tiles. Each wall mirrored the other perfectly with a detailed forest design that one could get lost in. The hot tubs were also decorated with the historic tile.

On a normal day, vampires and trusted humans mingled with each other in their secret oasis. Trusted humans scurried about at the beck and call of their vampire masters, as whispered conversations and sighs of ecstasy and pain floated through the air.

As Trent and Jerry entered the main hub of the Grotto with Molly and Tom in their arms, they were met with chaos and frenzied screams. The unmistakable scent of death and rot suffocated the air. Tables and chairs were reduced to splinters, while tapestries were shredded and covered in blood. Fresh flesh, body parts, and entrails glistened in the candlelight, as zombies and vampires alike feasted. Every few minutes, a horrifying scream reverberated throughout the Grotto as another human or vampire became infected.

Against her better judgment, the sweet succulence of blood and living flesh excited Molly. She squirmed in Trent's arms, desperate to be free. Her fangs unsheathed, ready to pierce soft, supple skin. Her teeth gnashed against the braided rope in her mouth, ready to tear into a meaty thigh or breast. She was *hungry*.

She screamed into the gag, eager for release.

Without a word, Jerry and Trent hid Molly with Tom's body behind the closest abandoned bar in the outbound tunnel. Again they ran into the throngs of ravenous undead—both human and vampire alike.

Molly sat behind the bar, facing Tom's body, and fought against her restraints. The skin around her wrists split in protest as blood trickled down her arms like a small river. For the moment, she stopped her useless struggle and listened to the world around her. The sound of tearing flesh, breaking bones, and smacking lips ignited her supernatural hunger. Irritated, she kicked Tom's body in the thigh with her bound feet. Not satisfied, she kicked him again and again. On the fourth kick, something fell out of his back pocket.

A knife made out of vampire teeth and bone.

Two rows of razor-sharp vampire teeth protruded on either side. The teeth, bonded to the bone with vampire blood, formed a six-inch blade. The handle of the knife, also carved vampire bone, added another three inches to the knife. To a casual observer, the knife looked like a disturbing comb.

Molly's excitement reached nirvana, as the scent of fresh blood swirled around her head. She reached for the knife and quickly removed herself from the restraints.

Behind the bar Molly stood, shoulder aching, wrists bleeding with bits of zombie flesh stuck to her zombie-blood splattered clothes. The pale white skin on her left arm was tattooed black with roping, twisting veins.

Chaos reigned supreme in the vampire city. In an instant, Molly jumped over the bar, out of the tunnel, and onto the platform as she stalked deeper into the chaos in search of fresh flesh. She took a deep breath—nothing but the stench of dead blood and dead meat. She stepped over miscellaneous body parts, pieces of shattered furniture, and even a zombie without arms and legs—his limbs torn from the trunk of his body when he was alive. His chest was ripped open, a hollow hole where his organs should be, his heart and lungs torn out by desperate and gouging fingers. He lay on his back, his dead brown eyes staring sightless at the concrete ceiling. His jaw worked mechanically as it waited for just one juicy morsel to pass through his lips.

"Poor bastard," Molly whispered. "At least you don't know what's happened to you."

Molly left him to bite at the air. Again, she inhaled.

Finally she caught the scent of glorious flesh—and fear.

The air suddenly filled with a full-bodied succulence. Molly followed the scent across the platform and down into the inbound tunnel and to another abandoned bar. The bar, like the one she and Tom had been stashed behind, was expansive. All the bars in the Grotto held every type of alcohol currently in production. The walls behind each of these bars held a door. Between the shelves of liquor and glasses there was a door hidden within the decoration of Rookwood tiles. The doors aren't immediately apparent until someone walks through. As Molly approached this particular bar in the inbound tunnel, she noticed that door quietly closing. The full-bodied succulence ended at the door as the latch softly clicked.

Molly leapt over the bar effortlessly and pressed an ear against the tiled door. Through the tile and wood, she heard a human heartbeat from within. Frightened, the heart pounded furiously against the human's ribcage. Molly inhaled. She lost the scent.

Cautiously, she opened the door.

Like the rest of the Grotto, this room was lit with candles in chandeliers. Only the table directly beneath the main chandelier was illuminated. Vampires couldn't see in pitch-blackness, but they didn't need much light to see, either. Molly's eyes quickly adjusted to the low level of light and could see every detail of the room perfectly, as if she stood directly beneath the sun.

The human, however, could not.

The scent of this human radiated out of her skin with each beat of her heart. The scent enveloped Molly in its essence like a warm comforting hug from her grandmother as it pulled her into the room.

She closed the door.

Molly was familiar with the room. It was a part of vampire life that she abhorred. In the corners of the room were cages large enough to fit five human women—all young. Those who were imprisoned were taken out of the cages and paraded onto the stage at the front of the room. Men—human and vampire—placed their bids, paid their money, and left by way of a private entrance on the other side of the room with their new human toy. The young women were never seen or heard from again.

Somewhere within, hiding in the shadows, a beating heart waited for her. The blood rushing through this person's veins sang to her while the scent of fresh meat begged her to dine. Molly shook with hunger and her blood raged; she could no longer wait to satiate her lust.

"Come out, come out, where ever you are."

Molly crept around the room, listening to the heartbeat. A few steps to the left, and it grew softer, and when she doubled back a few more steps to the right, the rhythm exploded in her ears.

And there she was. Hiding behind the steps that led to the stage.

Molly stood over the terrified woman. She recognized her as a trusted human servant to Bernie Shaw, a fledgling vampire still learning the ropes of his new eternal life.

Her name was Tiffany.

Tiffany, with long curly bright yellow hair that smelled of lavender and trusting blue eyes, recognized Molly and relaxed slightly. After all, the girlfriend of the vampire leader wouldn't harm a trusted human.

Molly smiled at the young girl.

The warring blood in her veins reached its peak as both the vampire and zombie infections screamed at her to eat while her heart and soul screamed for retreat. Not strong enough to resist her hunger, Molly succumbed to the blood as she reached for the terrified girl. Molly took her by the neck and brought her to her feet.

Tiffany didn't struggle.

Molly ripped into the girl's throat, chewing and drinking at the same time. The taste of Tiffany's flesh and blood sent Molly into euphoria. Thick, tangy, and warm, Tiffany's warm blood slid down Molly's throat like an oyster. She couldn't get enough. With her vampire speed, she took another bite, and another. Molly dug her fingers into Tiffany's flesh and muscle as she ripped it from the bone like string cheese. She ate and drank until there was nothing left of Tiffany but bone.

Triumphant, her blood rejoiced as she stood, soaked in the gore of a young girl.

Sucking droplets of blood from her fingers, Molly again was on the hunt for fresh meat.

She rushed out of the room and back into the chaos of the Grotto. Further down the platform, towards Court Street, Molly heard Trent scream in rage. She ran in his direction.

But at Race Street, she caught wind of another delectable scent. This time it was vampire. Pungent and savory, this vampire begged to be eaten. Without hesitation, Molly tackled him to the ground. She didn't take the time to look him in the eye as her fingers gouged into his flesh.

MOLLY NO!

Trent's voice inside her head made her pause for a brief second before she sunk her teeth into the vampire's succulent flesh. She tore his chest open as she shoved handfuls of skin and muscle into her mouth. The vampire shrieked in pain.

Before she could reduce him to bone, a hand tightened around her throat and tossed her across the platform.

Trent stood on the other side of that throw. His blue eyes looked into hers from across the distance, as sorrow claimed his beautiful face. In his left hand he held an ash-wood stake.

Please, Molly. Don't.

Knowing she would never be rid of her addiction to flesh, Molly charged. Teeth bared, hands out before her with claw-like fingers, she charged at Trent like a mad woman, hot tears threatening the edges of her eyes.

Trent raised the ash-wood stake and plunged it deep into Molly's brain.

Before the cold, overwhelming darkness drowned her, the last thing she saw were her lover's deep, ocean-blue eyes.

I loved you, Trent said in her mind. *And now I will fight this war without you.*

LONE

JOSEPH DUMAS

"The air breathes silence. The lights are out. The night sky and moon give an ambient darkness which has settled into my pupils nicely. I travel post-dusk due to the rabid freaks that lust after my flesh. The night lends me cover and their sight is weak. I move quietly and cautiously from place to place, finding shelter wherever it lay."

He prepares his gear after he finishes jotting some loitering thoughts into his haggard journal, which has been receiving entries for two years now, each signed with the initials FJ. He places the leather-bound book into his dirty backpack and takes a swig from an old metal bottle. The liquid drips from his bottom lip into his unkempt beard as he wipes his mouth and gets to his feet.

"Time to go," he mumbles to himself.

He steps out of the small shed he was holed up in for a little over a week. The dusk air blows against his face and carries a dead scent of decay and misery. Slowly, he moves down a dirt road, passing cars caked in dust and debris. Shadowy figures move about in the distance without noticing him.

Suddenly, lights come over the hill rapidly. He freezes in the middle of the road as the light reflects off his dirty skin and clothes. As he realizes more than the undead roam about on this night, his feet receive the message and he bolts to the nearest bush.

He dives into the brown leaves and slows his breathing. Two trucks screech as they stop and create a dirty cloud around them. A handful of grungy-looking people, three males and one female, step from the vehicles and each bear arms.

"We know you're there," one man says.

"Ha, come on out!" shouts the female as her high-pitch squeal carries through the night air.

FJ squats in the once-beautiful bush, his pupils darting back-and-forth at the seemingly hostile bunch of travelers. He holds his breath—something he can do for few minutes before getting lightheaded. He holds his legs still and steadies his weight as best as he can. As the strangers walk around the road, looking for any sign of him, he notices undead corpses stumbling toward the headlights, moaning. As he waits, he begins to feel his right foot sinking slightly. He looks down and sees that he is standing atop an old stick. The dried out twig was beginning to break. Then, the small snap echoes through the air as it seems to shake the earth.

"Get 'em!" one of the men shouts.

FJ lets out his held breath and quickly bolts away from the group.

"There he is!"

The undead walkers moan louder as the calls of the strangers arouse their sickly taste buds. FJ runs to the nearest house, quickly looking around for any signs of movement. As he nears a glass door on the side, a gunshot breaks through the air, smacking the eardrums of anyone in range.

FJ's calf explodes as the metal casing rips through his muscle and shatters against his bones. He lets out a cry as he falls forward and breaks through the glass door, landing in a pile of the broken glass and blood inside an average-looking living room.   He looks up and sees a couch and a recliner, both facing a television atop a nice-looking entertainment center. All of the items are covered in a thick layer of dust. Then, his eyes focus as he spots a rotting corpse sitting on the recliner with its head tilting back-wards. The skin appears to be once white, now a grayish brown. The skin looks sticky and without any fat or muscle. The body looks more like a skeleton with a worn-down leather sheet draped over it.

After observing the corpse, he looks back to see shadows of people, both living and dead, coming toward the house, silhouetted by the headlights. As fast as possible, he picks himself up, pushing shards of glass into the palm of his hands. He grunts at the pain and gets to his feet, only able to put pressure on one leg. As he starts limping through the house, a whistling breath comes from across the room. The corpse in the chair tilts its head forward and its jaw flaps open. The eyes of the creature stare at FJ, though they probably aren't functional as the pupils are all black. FJ can not discern if the corpse was once male or female because the level of decay is so high. Slowly, it reaches its hand toward FJ, but he wonders if the dead thing could even stand without its legs shattering beneath it.

He quickly looks away and limps down a hallway. There are three doors on each side and a big window at the end. He looks around and picks up a large pot of dirt, a dead plant within it. He lifts it above his head and throws it through the window, sending it outside and smashing the terracotta against the ground below. He moves to the window and attempts to pick himself up and over. Then, realizing his strength is not sufficient enough to make it, he looks for an alternative.

Another gunshot echoes through the house—they're inside and it seems that the leathery corpse had finally been put to rest.

Quickly, he runs to one of the doors and opens it. A small closet. He goes inside and sits atop a hard plastic bin full of linen. Then he takes out a lighter from his pack. He lights up the small room with the small flint-powered flame and shuts the door and bars it with an ironing board. He flips off the light and listens for a moment.

"Where'd he go?" asks one of the men.

"Look," says another. "It looks like he went through the window."

"Damn it."

Three more gunshots go off.

"Let's get out of here before more show up."

"Can't believe he got away."

"You're getting slow."

"I ain't eatin' in days. He would've made a good meal."

"Hmmph," one grunts as the voices start to dissipate.

FJ lets out a sigh of relief and leans back in the linen closet. Another night with barely any travel and it seems he has found his new hiding spot. He props up his lighter and takes out his journal once again.

"As the lights came over the hills, I knew that this night was occupied. I knew my travels were on hold once again. There were foul things about—but not just the undead. There were blood-thirsty living souls out there, too. I'm truly alone in this world, the last sane human with a pulse. I will not give up hope no matter how tempting it may be. I will eat my last can of food and drink my last gulps of water. I will find the promise land and prosper. I will."

-FJ

DEAD SALVAGE

DAN CIESIELSKI

The pickup truck rumbled along the old road before skidding to a halt in front of a derelict supermarket, the name long since faded beyond legibility.

Tyler, who'd been riding in the bed, kept a look out from behind the barrel of the swivel-mounted Browning M2 machine gun while two more men exited the cab and leapt into the bed with him.

The driver, Jordan, was about five foot ten and had a strong build. The passenger, Nathan was taller and slender, while Tyler seemed to dwarf them both.

It was a familiar routine that required nothing more than glances and grunts. The fiery sunset seemed to rend the clouds asunder, and in that familiar silence, not even birds sang.

Tyler swept the gun over the dark storefront while his companions rummaged within a wooden crate. Nathan and Jordan both equipped themselves from the stash of weapons they'd salvaged from the wasteland.

When they were finished, Nathan assumed control of the Browning while Tyler dove into the crate for his own guns. Before closing the box, Tyler and Nathan grabbed two black duffle bags and followed Jordan into the deserted store.

The sound of Nathan's rumbling stomach reminded them that their cause was desperate; they normally foraged during the day, but starvation decided for them. The evening hours were especially perilous, and with scant moments of daylight left, they had to be quick.

Tyler turned on a flashlight within the gloomy store as the trio brandished their weapons.

Nothing moved, but they refused to let their guard down; they'd learned that even if the situation seemed safe, they could be in terrible danger. Jordan led the way down the bare aisles; everything had already been looted. Tyler's hands trembled as the flashlight's beam quickly leapt from one bare shelf to the next. Even the puppy chow was missing. Where was the food?

Finally, they discovered the last bit of food in the building. Tyler's breath caught in his throat, and he trained the single cone of light on cans of beans and corn.

Nathan and Jordan frantically shoved the cans into their duffel bags. In another aisle, they managed to find a single case of water bottles with only a few bottles missing. Nathan ripped open the plastic case and tossed the water in the bags.

Cool sweat moistening his armpits, Tyler couldn't help but think how lucky they were.

A clatter in the next aisle startled them.

"Shit," Tyler muttered and habitually checked the safety on the magnum he held in his other fist.

They listened closely. The methodical, slow drag of feet lazily scraping across the floor turned the foragers' heads to the end of the aisle. No matter how many of them Tyler had to put down...

Nathan pumped his shotgun.

A figure emerged in the trembling pool of light. Tyler and the others were too familiar with the smell of death to differentiate it from their world, but they didn't need to smell it, anymore. They didn't need to see the rotten flesh of the corpse to know that their luck had run out.

Where there was one, there would be more.

More sole-scraping against the linoleum.

"We're already surrounded," Nathan pointed out.

Tyler nodded, "Thanks for that, Captain Obvious. Let's do what we do."

He shoved the flashlight into his mouth, leveled his weapon, and watched his hands jolt upward from the massive gun's blast. The bright light from the gunfire stained his retinas with dancing stars, but the resounding thump following his shot was all he needed to hear to know he hit the target.

The ruined supermarket was brightened by a maelstrom of war. Machine guns rattled as the three experienced survivors carefully aimed each bullet for a leering, shadowed skull. The living dead coalesced out of the aisles, seemingly materializing out of the abyssal darkness.

Tyler used the flashlight as his weapon so his comrades could find the targets. They backed up to the door, careful not to allow any flesh-hungry mouths to surprise them from the corners.

One bite was all it took, and the infection would spread. Tyler refused to let it happen to him. He'd witnessed the transformation too many times; he would do anything to survive.

Every time a walking corpse went down it seemed like two more replaced it. They funneled out of every aisle, dark, hungry shapes that hardly resembled the people they'd once been.

An outstretched hand seized one of the duffel bags and viciously wrenched it from Jordan's grip. The cans spilled and rolled across the floor.

Tyler cursed. The precious food they'd salvaged was about to be wasted. They'd risked their lives for nothing. Their lives were predicated on the idea of foraging for meager supplies as they traveled between hopeful destinations in their quest to survive.

The salvage was everything.

Outside at last, Tyler turned and sprinted to the truck, flinging himself into the bed. He quickly took position behind the Browning and leaned on the trigger, unleashing a thunderstorm of lead upon the dead army which filed out of the store after the trio. The vibrations from the recoil shook his body violently, but he maintained a steady sweep across the storefront while grinding his teeth. Corpses piled on top of one another as they were ripped to pieces by the onslaught of destructive power.

Jordan leapt into the driver seat while Nathan threw the food into the bed; Tyler continued to deliver a second death unto the seemingly never-ending crowd. Nathan stopped beside the truck, knelt, and fired into the skulls of any strays. The truck's engine roared to life and Nathan grabbed hold of the side mirror while placing a foot on the step.

The tires spun, kicking up gravel and dust as Jordan floored the gas pedal and spun the steering wheel. Nathan would be able to get inside the cab once they were a safe distance from their attackers. For now, he would just have to hang on tight. As they sped away, Tyler and Nathan continued to mow down the seemingly endless ocean of zombies.

Taking a quick look in the rearview mirror, Jordan watched as the masses became smaller and smaller. When he looked back at the road, his sense of relief vanished. Up ahead, someone had dug a ditch across the horizon. It was too late to turn around, too late to stop, too late...

"Hold on!" Jordan shouted.

In one instant, Jordan understood what he needed to do. He pushed the pedal to the floor and prayed that his old, rickety truck that had survived two wives and a zombie apocalypse would come through one more time.

Nathan and Tyler turned around just in time: their eyes widened and their mouths hung open in a silent scream. The remaining duffel bag leapt out of the bed.

The truck left the earth and seemed to hover in the air for a moment. Time seemed to slow down for the group as they fled across the gap. Tyler tightened his grip on the turret, Nathan clung to the side of the truck, and Jordan prayed. The ground seemed to greet them, slamming into the bottom of the vehicle.

Tyler lost his balance and collapsed in the metal bed. Nathan, however, was less fortunate: he lost his grip and rolled to a stop in the dirt. On his back, Tyler tried to shout, "Go back!" but his words were carried away by the rushing wind. Jordan, eyes wide, kept on driving as the sun slowly drooped below the horizon.

Jordan hollered, his heart pounding. "Hell yeah! Dukes of Hazard all the way! And we're still rolling baby, still rolling!"

The adrenaline surging through his veins, Jordan drove into the sunset.

Nathan rose to his feet and dusted off his clothes. His shotgun was nowhere to be found. He checked the two pistols that were tucked into the waistband of his pants. His friends would return for him; Tyler hated to leave people behind.

His left ankle burned with fresh pain. He was lucky to only have sprained it.

As the truck continued to amble away, Nathan's heart sank. What the hell was Jordan's problem?

Should he stay where he was? What if they didn't come back? He had to fend for himself; shelter was paramount. The undead would be nearly invisible in that lightless wasteland.

He searched around for the few bottles of water they'd salvaged from the supermarket. Nothing.

Walking inside the ditch, he chanced upon a mound of rocks that seemed to have been piled on top of one another. Listening to his instincts, he removed one rock from the pile, and then another. He began to uncover a cave entrance. Was the ditch some sort of protective measure for the cave?

It had to be better than nothing. With a pocketful of useless shotgun shells, he uncovered the entrance and stepped into the darkness.

The sun had fallen out of the sky, leaving the world to the mercy of a full moon and a company of stars.

Tyler's head buzzed from where he'd struck the bed during their flight over the ditch. The truck relentlessly drove into the night, while the swivel-mounted Browning bounced as if dancing to its own beat.

Hours later, Jordan stopped the truck in front of a gas station along the deserted stretch of dirt road. Tyler immediately leapt out of the bed and waited for the driver to step out. The safety on his magnum was off.

"What's your problem?" Tyler cautiously asked.

Jordan furrowed his brow. "The hell you talking about? You got a reason why that piece is in your hand?"

"Maybe," Tyler spat. "I figure you got a good reason why you didn't stop the truck. We left a man behind. Or didn't you know?"

A long, tense silence passed between them. Jordan's eyes flickered to the magnum. He licked his lips and said, "Nathan's bones are likely broken. You want to bring a wounded man along? How can we take care of him, even if he's alive? You need to think about this..."

"I have thought about it," Tyler curtly cut him off. "Have you?"

"We didn't exactly make out like bandits in there. How long before we starve? It'll be easier for just the two of us."

"And what happens if you decide there's enough for just one of us?"

Tyler applied slight pressure to the trigger. He was ready to make the move; he'd done it before. The lawless land left nothing to chance. The only law was survival. If you weren't ready to live, than you were ready to die.

Jordan kicked a rock beneath his feet. "What are your chances alone?"

"What're yours?"

"We've been through it, Tyler. Since the base."

"Nathan, too, but here we stand."

Jordan pursed his lips and nodded. "All right. So things have changed."

Everything had changed. For six months they'd been on the run together since their meager attempt to quarantine the infection failed.

Nathan, Jordan, and twelve other members of their National Guard unit had survived the attack, a horrendous, bloody moment that never left Tyler's nightmares. Slowly, their band fell apart as the walking dead and creeping paranoia claimed members of their crew.

All of them wanted to find their loved ones in the chaos, but the clogged roads and burning cities kept them away.

Now, there were three.

Tyler reminded him, "It's like I told you before: we stick together. It's the only thing that keeps us human. We take care of one another, or we're just like those things out there."

Jordan nodded. "Let's look around for some gas. We'll head back and pick him up. Dead or alive."

Tyler eased off the trigger.

"You're right," Jordan conceded. "I just got this fire in me when we jumped that ditch." He lovingly tapped the truck's rusted door. "She's been good to me, you know. Better than any woman I ever knew."

Tyler smirked and said, "She needs gas."

They swept the gas station and found it to be safe. Gasoline was hidden in the back room, and they were fortunate enough to find a few sponge cakes unopened.

Inside the truck, Tyler said, "He knows not to wander too far if he doesn't have to. Plus, the sun was setting, so he had to find shelter for the night. So the farthest he could have gone is a mile or two. There wasn't anything else north until this station and he was stuck in that ditch, so he either went east or west."

"Any idea who may've dug the ditch?" Jordan asked.

Tyler shrugged. "There was a huge mound of rocks not far from where he dropped. The more I think about it, the less natural they seemed. You've got this ditch and then a pile of rocks right in the middle of it...doesn't make sense."

Jordan turned the key. "Then that should be the first place we look for him. I just hope he can hold out till morning."

The man-made cave was dark and cold. There was nobody inside and the entrance was small—just tall enough to crouch through. There was even a rock inside the cave to roll into the opening.

The bone-chilling sound of the undead moaning outside floated through the walls, reminding Nathan that he was in grave danger. The crowd from the supermarket had been riled up, and they were hungry for warm flesh.

For the past hour or two, he'd been trying to break into a locked chest in the middle of the cave's single chamber. A rusty, three-digit combination lock held the lid firmly shut and was reset to 0-0-0 when he arrived. Too restless to sleep, he'd been going through every possible combination in order. His back ached from sitting hunched over and his fingers were numb; he was about to give up when a loud click popped the lid up.

"Wow, who makes the combination six-six-six?" Throwing back the lid, he took a look inside and found three things: a neatly folded piece of paper, a hand-held walkie-talkie, and a strange gun-shaped machine with all kinds of lights and tubes. Nathan picked up the paper and unfolded it to read the contents.

If you're reading this, then I'm most likely dead or a zombie. This chest contains my greatest inventions. They're only prototypes, but they're the best I could do with the materials I had available. Before the epidemic spread out of control, I was able to observe the infected victims. I was close to a cure when my lab was destroyed. With the research I was able to salvage, I made these two devices. One is a hand-held infection recognition device scanner. Turn it on and point the Molecular Transmitter antenna wherever you want and the screen will display an approximate number of infected and how far away they are.

Nathan reached into the chest and picked up the walkie-talkie device and found a switch on the side. He flipped it up and the thing started to hum and beep. A screen that looked like radar lit up with dozens of small red dots slowly inching from one side to the other. As he swept the device back and forth, different foes appeared on the screen to correspond with the ones on the other side of the rock wall. He continued reading the letter.

The device can find zombies through almost any material. The second device is a modified assault rifle. Since bullets have little to no effect on the enemy (depending on where you shoot them) I have created this. The Energized Degeneration Device requires electricity and has a cord that will plug into any socket in houses or vehicles and can also be hooked up with jumper cables to other sources of electricity. Three batteries are strapped to it and should each hold a charge for 10 minutes before needing to be recharged. Just aim and shoot. The stronger the source of electricity, the more devastating the results will be.

The signature on the bottom of the page was illegible, but who made the two machines no longer mattered. Nathan reached down into the chest once more and pulled out the futuristic gun. It was more or less an assault rifle with a slender hose protruding from both sides of the barrel, coming back and reconnecting to the gun at the back of the stock.

From there, a cable extended out with a single, slender pronged end. Lights lined the top of the weapon, and on the right side of it, three cylindrical containers were strapped on.

An ardent lover of guns, Nathan had never seen anything like it. And if he saw Tyler and Jordan again, the weapon belonged to him. After all, anything a man could salvage could define a man's personal wealth.

Nathan felt like a king.

Curious, Nathan removed one of the cylinders and found that the hole where the magazine would normally go had been modified to fit the battery. He loaded the gun and it instantly reacted. One of the eight lights lit up with a dim, yellow glow.

Picking up the scanner, Nathan checked the surrounding area. Their numbers were dwindling, but there were a handful nearby. Carefully, he removed the boulder from the entrance of the cave and made his way out, making sure his pistols were loaded and the safeties off.

He slung the shotgun over his shoulder, eager to test the new weapon. He emerged through the cave's mouth—a zombie with its back turned stood twenty feet from Nathan's left. He lifted the modified assault rifle. Taking aim, he squeezed the trigger. Lights traveled through the tubes on the sides and the tip of the barrel glowed softly.

The creature slowly began to turn.

Suddenly, a visible pulse, less than five feet in diameter, fired out of the gun at incredible speed. When it passed through the unsuspecting zombie, the monster seemed to turn to dust. The rotten flesh sloughed off and the bones disintegrated. Not even the torn up clothes remained; everything was vaporized.

Nathan almost dropped the gun in utter disbelief. "What was that?" He looked down at the weapon in his hands, "I don't know who made you or how, but you are one epic machine." A noise behind him caught his attention and he pivoted with the gun raised.

Another corpse lingered just on the rim of the ditch. The slowly emerging day brightened the night with streaks of blue, and the limpid corpse seemed a foul silhouette—a featureless, putrid shadow.

Nathan pulled the trigger again and watched another pulse emanate from the tip of the weapon. Just like the first, his foe disintegrated.

"I think I'm going to like this gun," he declared, unable to stop the smile from spreading across his face.

It didn't take long to reach the ditch that had caused the separation in the first place. Spotting the pile of rocks Tyler had mentioned last night, Jordan adjusted his direction and they stopped five yards from the mound. Turning off the engine, Jordan grabbed a submachine gun from the passenger seat and exited the vehicle, while Tyler kept watch from behind the Browning as dawn approached.

The area seemed quiet, far too quiet for comfort. Jordan said, "Looks like our boy ran off."

Tyler shook his head. "He couldn't have gone too far without shelter; he was almost out of ammo. There can't be many places to hold up for a night within walking distance."

"We'll make a loop and see what we can find. Hopefully he'll turn up, but we have to take into account the alternative."

Tyler sighed. "I know, let's just try to find him."

Jordan took less than two steps back towards the truck when one of the rocks at the bottom of the mound moved to the side. "Look out!" Tyler shouted while he fixed the turret on the rocks before the words left his mouth.

Out of the cavernous hole emerged Nathan. He dusted himself off and squinted his eyes in the bright light, "What's up guys? I don't know about you, but I had a horrible night."

Jordan took a step in his friend's direction and cleared his throat. "You all right?"

Nathan frowned. "Starving, actually. I'm surprised you actually came back for me. You'd have more supplies between the two of you. It's not easy to split breadcrumbs three ways."

Tyler quickly intervened to prevent the seeds of distrust from being buried further into their hearts. "We need to continue to salvage. It's useless to go back into the town where we found the supermarket. There's another town not too far from here. We've got enough gas for the trip."

Nathan seemed to accept it. He was always willing to defer to Tyler, and he preferred to avoid confrontation. Nathan was a good man. Tyler believed he could trust him, and Nathan's presence could restore some balance within their fragile group.

Jordan crouched near the rim of the ditch and extended his hand.

"Wait! Nobody move yet." Tyler didn't want to take any chances. They'd been separated for a long time; anything could've happened overnight.

Jordan understood the situation and reached into his jacket pocket, pulling out a tennis ball. Tyler had done the same thing and the two extended the bright, yellow spheres in front of them.

The system was originated after what happened to their friends Frank and Andy. Frank had been infected, but nobody knew it. He was always joking around—trying to lighten the mood—so nobody noticed when he started acting weird. They thought he was just joking again. Once he started snacking on Andy, it was clear that he wasn't joking around. Frank was gone and it was too late for Andy.

The remaining three came up with the tennis ball idea. One of the first things to happen to an infected human is the loss of memory. Why would a zombie hold on to a tennis ball? It has no purpose whatsoever and would get left behind; but a human can remember to keep it with them at all times so that if ever separated, they can show that they kept the meaningless object because they remembered the plan: the plan to present the object to their friends to prove they are *not* infected.

Jordan and Tyler aimed their weapons at Nathan, waiting for his next move. If he still had his tennis ball, they would feel safe around him. If not, they would have no choice but to shoot their lost friend and move on.

Reaching into his pocket, Nathan searched, but had nothing. Trying a different pocket, he came up with the same result. Tyler and Jordan shared a quick glance and silently agreed to allow one more chance to retrieve the ball. Aware that he was running out of time, Nathan patted down his body, searching for the object that could save his life. "Wait, I have it! I know I have it. Just give me a second." He reached into two pockets and pulled out an empty hand. In the other hand, he held a dirt-encrusted tennis ball.

Jordan and Tyler loosened their hold on the weapons and welcomed their companion.

"Ready for more fun?" Jordan extended his hand again.

"Give me a second; I need to grab some things." Nathan hurried back into the hole.

Giving a quizzical look to Tyler, Jordan asked, "What could he need to grab?"

As quickly as he disappeared, Nathan reappeared holding a gun that looked like it came straight from a cheesy space movie, and a folded piece of paper. Before anyone could ask a question, he said, "I'll explain later, let's just go." Without wanting to waste more time, the three piled into the truck and drove off; a cloud of dirt trailing behind them.

There was one thing Nathan didn't show them.

Nathan explained the chest and the inventions he found inside. Tyler and Jordan were skeptical, but with the promise of a demonstration in the near future, they didn't question his claims. They drove all day, only stopping to fill the tank with gas. By the time the sun was setting again, they were ready to drop from exhaustion, starvation, and dehydration.

Time was running out. If they didn't salvage anything from the town, their chances were slim.

On the outskirts of the town, a gun shop sat quietly. For one evening, it would serve as the perfect base as night threatened to fall.

Jordan and Nathan approached the store with caution while Tyler, once again behind the Browning, swept the surrounding area for unwanted guests. Dust rolled through the cracked avenue.

The sleepy town would have been sparsely populated in its time, but hunting had been a popular and important aspect of the citizens' lives before they'd all been eaten or infected by the undead plague. The gun store had likely been a focal point in the local economy.

The faint smell of rot was carried by the wind, and once again, Tyler's stomach quaked hungrily.

Nathan glanced at the corpse radar. A single dot suggested that one corpse was within the shop. When the device was pointed a few yards down the road, a cluster of dots filled the screen.

Should he show his allies the radar? It could be of use to them, but still...

Jordan looked at the strange new gun with lusty eyes. It was only a matter of time before one of them tried to pry it from his hands. The radar should remain his secret. After all, it was his loot.

Checking to make sure his experimental weapon was loaded with a fresh battery, Nathan kicked in the door and readied the barrel at chest level—nothing. He waved the 'all clear' signal.

Tyler dismounted from the back of the truck and slung an assault rifle across his back. He couldn't help but notice the irony of their situation: they were well-stocked with firepower, but they could still die from hunger.

The front of the store was completely empty—all of the guns were gone. The trio walked into the back offices and storage room, and found each room as empty as the last, though the storage room contained boxes of left-behind ammunition. Nathan found the manager's office and stood outside of the door with his new-fangled gun leveled.

At first glance, the room seemed devoid of enemies, but past experiences had proven that first glances couldn't be trusted. Nathan advanced and jumped back instantly. From behind the desk, a decaying body crawled towards the intruders; the creature dragged its entrails and spinal cord along the floor, and glanced upward at them, its lips curled back over teeth that were cloaked by the shadows.

With years of experience, Nathan adjusted his aim and unleashed one of the deadly pulses, disintegrating the monstrosity instantly.

Jordan and Tyler leapt back in utter disbelief. "What the hell was that?"

"I know; it's pretty awesome."

The empty gun store was completely clear. Jordan took advantage of the moment to complain. "Crap, what now? I haven't eaten all day; I'm starving."

Tyler looked through the window. "We're here to do a job, we might as well do it. The two of you should roll out and look around."

Jordan protested. "No, we can't split up again."

"We need food and there isn't any here. And if something happens when we go looking for some, wouldn't it be nice to come back to a place that you know is safe and not have to recheck the entire building? Besides, how difficult can it be to protect a gun shop? It's not like I need to worry about running out of ammunition."

Nathan agreed with the plan. "He's right. Besides, we won't take very long. I'm sure we'll run into more trouble than he will."

Jordan nodded. "Fine, but no longer than twenty minutes." Jordan and Nathan returned to the truck, armed with their newly acquired gun and radar. Closing the door tightly behind them, Tyler re-checked his magnum.

After five minutes of silence, he began to grow bored and grabbed a hunting knife stored in an open safe under the cash register. He used the knife to draw a makeshift dartboard on one of the walls. Pacing five large steps away, he turned and aimed, throwing the knife with precision. The blade embedded itself an inch deep, slightly to the left of the center target.

He walked up, pried it out, and repeated the process four or five times before a noise outside caused him to hesitate. It sounded again, this time a little louder. Setting the knife down on a table, he walked to the window with his gun in hand and peeked through; twenty yards out was a human figure limping towards the store. Its jerking, ragdoll movement was a clear indication that it wasn't alive.

Sticking the tip of his gun out the window, Tyler took aim and dropped the creature with one round to the skull. The noise would surely bring more. He instantly regretted that he'd sent Jordan and Nathan away with the truck. What was he thinking? He'd disobeyed his own survival code—they were supposed to stick together.

At that moment, a loud crash echoed from the back of the building. Whipping around, Tyler sprinted to see what the commotion was.

The back wall had collapsed, and an army of groaning undead foes spilled in through the opening. Drawing the assault rifle, he unloaded clip after clip into the advancing wave. Every time one fell, another zombie was there to take its place.

There were too many for the magnum to be useful. The assault rifle clicked emptily, and Tyler turned tail and ran into the storage room, cursing himself for not taking stock of the ammo before.

The laws of survival in the wasteland were absolute. Tyler had broken them.

The town was far too quiet. It was the first thing Jordan and Nathan noticed when they arrived: there's no activity anywhere. Not a single zombie in sight.

Nathan asked, "So are we just extremely lucky or is this the calm before the storm?"

He was careful to check the radar without Jordan noticing.

"Have we *ever* been lucky?" Jordan asked.

"Actually, yes. You and Tyler were lucky enough to jump that ditch. And I was lucky enough to find this." Nathan lifted his gun into the air.

Jordan glanced at the weapon.

"You know," Nathan pressed, "I never thanked you for coming back. You wasted a lot of gas. Did both of you think it was a good idea, or just you? I know you've got a good heart, but I wonder about Tyler, sometimes."

The truck skidded to a halt in front of a family owned pharmacy.

"Let's do the job," Jordan said coldly.

They rushed inside and ransacked the shelves. Nathan yelled, "Jackpot!" as he quickly collected a few spare cans of spam. Nathan glanced at the radar—time was growing short. He rushed back outside with his salvage, while Jordan followed behind, his arms full of cans and bottled water.

Inside the truck once again, they sped back to the temporary base. Nathan was immensely pleased. He had it all. *Almost.*

Nathan said, "We've got food, and you want to go back for Tyler? You really are an admirable man."

"What are saying?" Jordan's eyebrows darted up.

"I'm just glad that we're friends."

Everything suddenly became clear to Nathan. At last, he understood what he needed to do in order to survive. Tyler's righteousness had been the wrong way of doing things.

The truck skidded to a stop in front of the gun store, and they sprinted to the door and pounded on it. The door swung open on squeaky hinges.

They tightened their grips on their guns and surveyed the room. In the tense silence, a ball bounced along the floor and rolled against his boot. Jordan picked it up and held it at eye level. It was a yellow tennis ball.

Nathan stood outside of the store with the futuristic weapon pointed at Jordan. He withdrew his own ball then and bounced it into the store.

"Won't be needing it," Nathan said. "By the way, I forgive you."

Jordan put his hands up over his head. "Please, no. Wait..."

Tyler appeared from behind Jordan: his clothes, his face, his height and build, but not *him*.

His skin had a sickly green tint to it; stark white bone poked out of his flesh, while his clothes were soaked in blood. As Jordan turned, Tyler's mouth opened wide, and his teeth bore down on the back of Jordan's skull.

Nathan said, "Call me Captain Obvious, but it looks like we shouldn't have split up." He squeezed the trigger and set free one of those devastating pulsations from his beloved piece of salvage.

THE ZOMBIE WARCRAFT GUILD

T. FOX DUNHAM

I miss aspects of the old world: electricity, clear highways, playing World of Warcraft every night after work. After our guild fled the city, we suffered game withdrawal.

By the second week, Philly reeked like rancid road kill seven days in the sun and all sticky. The fact that most of the population had been eaten or infected with the Helsinki-221 virus made residency undesirable.

At least, I got to play Warcraft everyday for a while. When FEMA declared a national emergency and the military imposed martial law, I enjoyed some of the best weeks of my life. I had a crate of Ramen in the closet and enough bottled water to last for a while, but I couldn't get a Big Gulp, since 7-11 and Cedar Avenue had turned into a war-zone.

It was a dream come true. My work in the IT department at Moose-Shoes killed my brain cells everyday from nine to six. The bus got me home to my building by seven, and I'd only have a couple of hours to play. My gaming guild, 'Run Clìar,' raided on Thursday nights, but I always had to log off by eleven, usually missing the last raid boss. Fox named the guild after an old Irish phrase. It loosely translated into, 'veteran warriors and friends.' I'd started a shaman, planning to raid-heal, but I had no time to level it.

Some nights I dreamed I existed in the World of Warcraft, where a troll lived by his sword or wand, off the land, a free realm without the need to draw a salary or pay the rent. A society based on trade was contrary to the human, animal condition. It caused mass depression, and people shoved handfuls of Zoloft and Lyrica into their mouths to try to restore the balance. Unfortunately, I couldn't get down to Rite Aid to fill my Zoloft prescription.

For twenty straight days, we played Warcraft, while riding out the zombie plague. The guild hung out on voice-chat and had group discussions on the best ways to secure our homes. Half of the guild members were ex-military, and we'd all been planning for the upcoming zombie war for years: talking about our fantasies, even role-playing them out with dice. We were prepared. We secured our doors, made sure we had points of exit, like my fire escape down from the sixth floor of my building. We used headphones and just laid low while the undead conquered the streets. After all, eventually the U.S. Military would take the country back and things would go back to normal. That's usually how the movies ended anyway.

But I didn't want it to end. I *capped* my shaman's level. I didn't think I'd have so much fun raid-healing, but I lived a lot longer in game than playing a melee toon, especially during boss fights.

By the second week, the power fluctuated. Most internet search engines started coming up *Website Not Found*, but Warcraft stayed live. We even noticed a difference in the gaming population. Random groups for dungeons took longer to form. Healers became rare, and my shaman became popular; players paid me the kind of obsequious attention they usually did when they discovered a female who played the game. I just figured we'd play until society sorted itself out.

"Power's going to stay on for maybe a couple more days," Khagrim said over voice-chat. "After that, it's not coming back. Stone age."

"We've got nuclear power," Mortee grumbled at his brother. "The army will keep it running."

"The army's wiped out or hiding in bunkers," Khagrim snapped back.

Mortee replied with his usual eloquence: "Rabble. Rabble. Rabble."

"I had to stuff wet rags in my windows and under the door to keep out the smoke," I said. "Philly is burning."

"Same here, Grok," Khagrim added.

I'd named my *toons* after the Martian meditation technique known as grokking, from Heinlein's book, *Stranger in a Strange Land.*

The Dude, Kerani, Khagrim, Mortee and Fox, the guild leader, also lived in Philly. We used to roleplay at Pyramid Comics. The group kept together when we started playing online games.

"It's only a matter of tick-tocks till the conflagration spreads," Fox said, still retaining his British accent that made us all feel safe and in good hands. "Gentleman, ever read Albert Camus' *The Plague*?"

Voice-chat silenced.

Fox sighed. "Quick *Fox* version then," he said. "If you can't change when life changes, you die. If we're not burned to death, the zombies are going to start massing into the buildings, searching for food. We have a small window here. Gentleman, fellow guild members, loyal friends and brother warriors, it's time to make our exodus. Dude, can you arrange transportation? Khagrim, do you own any weapons after your military service?"

"I've been plating my Dodge truck with aluminum sheets," Dude said. "I welded spikes on the front hood. Lansdale's not too bad yet, so I could get some extra gas. We could do this."

"I've got an M-1 rifle, some handguns and ammo," Khagrim said.

"Here's the plan," Fox said, the confidence in his voice putting me at ease. "Dude. Get your truck built. Kerani and I live in Lansdale, so he can grab us first. Grok, we'll get you next since you can leap off your fire escape. Pack up what medical supplies you have from the paramedic training courses you took. What's the undead situation in your streets?"

I took off my headphones, looked down through the living room window. A couple of *bodies* staggered around, but we could avoid those. I reported.

"I'm not going," Mortee said. "I'm going down with Warcraft."

"Don't be such a dumbass," Khagrim said.

"Rabble. Rabble. Rabble."

"I respect your decision, Mortee," I said. "You want to die how you lived, glued to your mouse and casting fire bolts from your Warlock. I salute you."

Dude drove the back alleys, banging up his truck at times. He plowed into the few *bodies*, running them through with the spikes mounted to the grille. A woman missing both arms dangled off one of the spikes, impaled through her chest.

I leapt from the fire escape ladder and landed in the back of the truck. Fox sat up in the front, wearing his tan fedora hat. Kerani squeezed in the middle. She held a table leg, bloody after being used as an improvised club.

"Good to have you, Grok," Fox said, extending his hand through the cabin's back window.

We plowed through South Philly, stopped in front of Khagrim's house. Bodies surrounded it. He tossed us the bag of guns then jumped off his roof and hit the side of the truck, snapping his leg. He tumbled into the back.

"Move your ass!" Khagrim yelled, holding his leg, his face filled with pain. The Dude sped us out of there just as zombies mobbed the truck. Mortee saluted us through his bedroom window. We returned the salute to our comrade who had honored the guild with his life. He sat back down at his PC and resumed questing.

"Hell of a bloke," Fox said. "I regret I never made him a guild officer."

"He just wanted it so he could kick Khagrim out of the guild," I said.

"There dies one of the great smart-asses of our time," Kerani eulogized.

We rode in silence through the city.

I checked Khagrim's leg and took out a brace from my bag, then some bandages. I wanted to be a paramedic, but I washed out of the course. The sight of blood turned my stomach.

"This is gonna hurt," I told him. I snapped the bone in place. I also gave Kerani some rubbing alcohol and bandages for a bleeding gash on The Dude's arm. The wound was already turning black.

Khagrim handed Fox two daggers with ornate handles. Fox grinned when he accepted them—the weapons of a rogue, his class on Warcraft.

We no longer used our given names. That world had died and reanimated. We had to leave it behind to survive, just like the book Fox had mentioned. I planned to read it. I had plenty of time to read now.

We barreled through the streets, more undead amassing around the truck. We had to get out of Philly.

"Walt Whitman Bridge," Fox said. We followed our liege. Looking at his calculating eyes, I could see how he'd earned his cunning moniker.

Once we hit I-95, abandoned cars blocked the way. The Dude navigated the shoulder, though he lost a headlight in a tight pass. We had to slow down. Khagrim shot the zombies that got too close to the truck. A parade of undead surged behind us, snowballing as we got closer to the bridge. Up ahead, I could see the blue scaffolding of the bridge over the Delaware River, leading to safety in

New Jersey, though we'd still have to get out of Camden and into the country. Over the radio, we'd heard tell of a safe zone in Ocean City, New Jersey. They'd blown their causeways and bridges leading across the bay.

We hit the bridge, got about halfway using the empty, opposite lane that normally traversed with traffic heading into the city. The Dodge slammed into the divider. The Dude clawed at Kerani, green ichor oozing from his lips. It hadn't dawned on me he might have been bit. We all had to learn new rules for a new world, the World of *Zombiecraft*.

Fox brandished his daggers. For a minute, he truly resembled his elf rogue. I held The Dude by his neck through the window. Fox hesitated.

"Kill him!" Kerani yelled, struggling with The Zombie Dude.

"But he's such a good tank," Fox replied. Then he realized there was no choice and he drove both daggers into The Dude's eyes.

The undead moved in on us. Khagrim fired off his M-1. I grabbed a .45 and fired into the crowd, hitting bodies mostly in the chest and arms, but keeping them back. I hate melee combat. It was only a matter of time until we *wiped*, and Khagrim and I would be first.

"Kerani, get out," Fox ordered. "Khagrim will cover you."

Kerani, our other raid-tank, yelled a battle cry. She climbed over Fox and charged out of the truck, holding her club high. She knocked a zombie's head clean off and into the river.

"*One-shotted* him!" I yelled over the gunfire.

"Stay on the tank's target," Fox reminded us. "Don't *aggro* the others." Khagrim took out the undead that clawed at her. She got around the truck and pulled the driver's door open. Fox kicked The Dude's corpse out, dumping him off the side of the bridge.

"Farewell, Dude" Fox said, rubbing a tear from his eye. The Dude always gave his damage buffs to Fox—a strong bond in the game.

The undead surrounded the back of the truck. We couldn't fire fast enough to keep them down.

Kerani jumped in and put the truck in drive, then floored it.

"Nicely done, guild," Fox said. My chest tingled whenever our leader patted us on the shoulder. "Once we reach Ocean City, we'll contact Coredelia, Anubis, Dancingbear, Korombos and the rest, maybe even go after them. We've always made a formidable raiding group. We'll survive."

Khagrim's shock had worn off, and he grimaced from the pain in his leg.

"We need to stop once we're out of the urban areas, hit a pharmacy and grab some pain killers," I said. "Some antibiotics, too."

I really enjoyed playing a healer.

REVELATION / REJUVENATION

ALYN DAY

Her expression was calm, perhaps it could even have been considered serene. Her eyes, a clear, cool blue on which she was often complimented, were half open, almost sleepy-looking. Her lips were parted slightly and her pale blond hair waved gently, as if being kissed by a warm breeze. But Stacey Traymore wasn't alive any longer.

Stacey was behind the wheel of her little red car at the bottom of Trenchmoor Lake, and her boyfriend, Steven Stearns, was the one responsible.

Steve loved Stacey, he really did. But when push came to shove, there was no one Steve Stearns loved more than himself. Dating a reporter was supposed to have been good for his image. He had imagined that getting on Stacey's good side would gain him all sorts of perks, such as access to insider information on what was going on in the bio-med industry, favorable coverage for his own operation, Polystar Labs, and maybe even the chance to seed Stacey's news outlet with stories of his own.

He had gotten those perks, but what he hadn't counted on was Stacey's growing interest in exactly what was being developed at Polystar, and whom it was being sold to. He had caught her snooping through his things one too many times, and that had been the end of Stacey Traymore.

He remembered her expression when he'd caught her riffling through the gym bag he'd hidden the samples he'd absconded with. The pretty pink 'O' of surprise her mouth had formed, the way her expression had shifted to one of innocent concern rather than the guilt he knew underlined it. The bright red pearl of blood on the tip of her finger from where she'd cut herself on a slide when he'd walked in on her unexpectedly.

No one's perfect, Steve thought. So what if he'd wanted to make a little extra money on the side. Was that so bad? He hadn't thought so, especially not when a researcher from a leading cosmetics company had offered him thirty million in advance for a sample of the tissue rejuvenation serum his division was developing. What was the harm? Tests on the solution itself had been inconclusive at best. The researcher would be given a sample of diluted serum which may or may not even work, and in exchange Steve could pad his nest egg a bit. All things considered, not too bad a deal. That was until Stacey had had discovered emails between Steve and the cosmetics rep. Steve saw nothing particularly wrong with what he was doing, but if it were to get out, it had the potential to end his career, maybe even land him in jail.

Stacey couldn't be allowed to put that information in print. It would ruin him. He briefly debated talking to her, trying to reason with her, but that part of his brain was quickly overruled by his own sense of self-preservation. Stacey knew too much. Simply put, she couldn't be allowed to live.

Steve had worked quickly. He had planned for this, after all. Ever since that first time he'd seen her interest pique at the mention of the project he was working on, he'd thought about what to do if things got out of hand and Stacey became a problem that had to be dealt with. Steve had smiled as he entered the room, his jovial tone and easy going attitude completing his deceit flawlessly. If Stacey had a clue about what was going to happen next, she'd given no indication.

"Stacey, honey," Steve had smiled, really pouring it on, "How are you this evening?" Stacey had continued to smile as she stood up. "Oh hi, Steve. Listen, have you seen my gym bag? I thought this was it, but I must've been mistaken."

"Nope," Steve had shrugged, continuing the charade. "Haven't seen it." He'd moved closer to his pretty girlfriend, maintaining his calm, good-natured attitude.

Stacey had seemed a bit nervous, but it was probably just because she'd been worried about being caught. He'd put his arm around her shoulders and led her out of the room. "Stacey, what do you think about going out for dinner tonight? How about that Italian place you like over on Pearl Street?"

Her eyes had lit up. "Oh that sounds lovely. Let me get my coat." Just as she'd turned, Steve had darted forward and snapped her pretty neck in one swift motion. Her lifeless body had crumpled to the floor in front of him.

He'd smiled, thinking to himself how easy it had been. He'd picked Stacey up and carried her limp form out to her car. Looking down at her innocent face, she looked as if she'd been sleeping off a late-night in the back seat rather than preparing to meet her watery grave. Steve had gotten behind the wheel and closed the driver's door, glancing back as he did so. Had he imagined he'd seen her hand twitch? No, it was just nerves, he'd told himself, and the wavering light filtering in through the wet glass from the recent rainstorm.

It was less than a mile drive to Trenchmoor Lake, and just around the corner from the little condo the couple had shared. Not a long walk at all, and with any luck, the rain would obscure the tire tracks left by Stacey's car and he could report her missing the next day. He'd claim she'd just never gotten home from work. Nodding and smiling at himself and his cleverness in the rearview mirror, he hadn't felt the slightest hint of guilt about what he planned to do, what he had done, to the woman he was supposed to love.

When he arrived at the lake, it had begun to rain again, and the surface of the water was roiling as rain fell. He'd gotten out of the car and lugged Stacey gracelessly out of the backseat and slid her in behind the steering wheel and put the transmission into drive. Before he'd closed the door, he'd paused to kiss her lifeless cheek and then went behind the car to help push it into the churning water. He stood and watched as it sank from view before making the short walk home.

Several feet below the frothing surface, the lake was calmer. The water was clear and cool. Fish darted past the car's windshield, their muted colors accented by small bursts of silver as the thin, pale light caught their scales. Stacey sat in the driver's seat like a broken doll. Her head was canted slightly to the side on her broken neck.

A thin, reedy little stream of blood rose up from her cut finger, like a whiff of smoke from a blown-out birthday candle. In the cold and darkness of Trenchmoor Lake, Stacey's eyes blinked once, twice. Her hand twitched and soon she was climbing out of the car and making her way to the surface. Steve had a good head start, but she would catch him soon enough.

REJUVENATION

My chest is burning; my lungs feel like they're on fire. My brain feels fuzzy, disconnected, like it would slosh around in my skull if I tried to move my head. The ache in my respiratory system is becoming unbearable. Suddenly it occurs to me that I need to breathe. I take a deep breath and feel cold water rushing into my mouth and nose, down my throat to cool the fires within me. The feeling is not unpleasant.

I try to open my eyes for several minutes before I realize that they *are* open, and it's simply too dark for me to see anything. The burning feeling in my chest is gone now, replaced by a heavy sort of iciness, as if a block of cool granite has replaced my internal organs. My limbs feel heavy and stiff. It's an effort just to lift my hand. I try to flex my fingers but they don't react as I expect them to, the movement is slow and sluggish and very slight, more like a twitch than anything else. I bring them close to my face and can barely make out their pale shapes against the backdrop of velveteen darkness that seems to have fallen all around me. Where am I?

How did I get here? I try to sigh, but even that small movement is too much for me and the tendons and joints in my back pop and strain in protest. The notion that I'm breathing water doesn't seem odd or alarming to me, nor does the realization. I know, somehow, that those things *should* mean something to me, but they simply do not. I feel very matter of fact about it.

Once more I try to move my hand. This time it responds just a hair more urgently, just a touch quicker. My fingers curl in on themselves like the legs of a dead spider. With great, halting effort, I turn my head. I see a door. I'm in my car. Trapped. In water. The lake. Was I driving? Was I drunk? It doesn't matter now. None of it matters. What matters is getting free and getting home to Steve.

Steve.

His research project. That's what I was working on; the last thing I remember. Sneaking into his office and looking around for the samples he pilfered from Polystar Labs, where he worked as a research scientist. The gym bag. I remember a black gym bag, full of wadded up newspapers and a little black case containing a few vials and a dozen sets of slides. One of them cut my hand when Steve walked in.

Steve. Some kind of serum.

He was working on some kind of serum to rejuvenate dead tissue.

Sell it.

He was going to sell it to someone from Chloë Cosmetics. Thirty thousand dollars. I'd have asked for twice that much. Steve has no spine. Going to take the samples myself. Blackmail. I'd have a hundred grand in my hands right now if Steve hadn't…

Steve. He was probably home right now while I sit trapped in my car at the icy bottom of Trenchmoor Lake. When I flex my fingers again, this time they listen. This time they obey. I stretch my arms as much as I'm able in such a confined space. It isn't much, but it is enough to loosen them up a bit, get the blood flowing, so to speak. I flex my toes and stretch my ankles. I reach up and place a hand on either side of my head and do my best to realign my poor, broken neck.

There is a crunching sound and a scraping of bones against one another but then all is silent and my head is more or less straight. My tongue feels like a dead lump of clay in my mouth, which I suppose isn't far off from the truth. Despite this, I'm hungry. I'm famished. I'm ravenous. My stomach is like a bottomless pit, a spinning, swirling black hole of a chasm which nothing can ever fill. I snatch at a little lake fish as it swims past me. It squirms in my hand until I shove it into my mouth and bite down. It feels good. Warm. Salty. Tasty. Dinner.

Steve. He said he was going to take me to dinner. My favorite restaurant. Il Pomodoro. Red clam sauce over angel hair pasta. My favorite dish. It doesn't sound at all appetizing to me now, despite the hunger gnawing at my guts, threatening to turn them inside out with its ferocity. I look around for another fish, but don't see one. They must have seen what had happened to their brother and fled the vicinity. I swallow and feel sharp fish bones sliding around in my stomach. I look around before remembering that I can pull the door handle and get out.

The door opens slowly and I have to shove it as hard as I can, but eventually it gives and I float to the surface in a cloud of nibbling little guppies that dart away from my clutching fists. My movements are still slow and sluggish but at least my body seems to be reacting more or less the way I'd expect it to.

After a few moments, my head breaks the surface and I bob along the water like a buoy. Water runs from my nostrils, but I barely register it. I'm not far from the shore. I push forward, feeling like I am swimming through quicksand rather than the lake where Steve and I spent our summers, laughing and sunning ourselves on its manmade shores. Another life. Another me. A girl I couldn't contend with.

I pull myself forward through the lake until my feet touched the bottom. I drag myself to the shore, feeling the sandy silt beneath me give way as I lurch across it. Slowly, I stand up. I feel the weight of eons pressing down on me as water drips and drains.

In the cool blue moonlight, I look down at myself. My flesh looks thick and spongy. I make a fist and it squelches, rivulets of water running down my arm. My skin feels tight and bloated. Numb. I lift my head. I can smell something…delicious. The most mouthwatering scent I have ever inhaled fills my nose. I make my way towards the highway.

Home seems a very different place to me somehow. The lights are all on and my sister's car is in the driveway. I pick up the little ceramic toad sitting next to the front walk and search for the hide-a-key slot on its bottom. It takes me a few tries, the skin on my finger tips coming a bit loose and peeling away before I get it free, but eventually I do. I let myself inside. Steve is sitting at the kitchen counter, the phone to his ear, as my sister stands over his shoulder, looking pensive. They both look up when I enter, still dripping fetid lake water. They don't look happy to see me.

THEY

JOE FILIPPONE

Choppers overhead. Screams twenty-four seven. Gunfire. Explosions. Growls. Sirens. Helpless pleas. That was the chorus of Hollywood now ever since "They" invaded.

New York was the first city to fall.

They came out of the sewers. Hundreds of them. Thousands. No one bothered to count. The news speculated that They must have been down there for years. Hiding. Plotting. Growing stronger. Waiting for the right time to attack. After They raped New York, They made their way west, recruiting more minions for their demonic army and killing every innocent who stood in the way. We didn't stand a chance.

Watching the news, when there still was news to watch, was like watching a horror movie. Cities were littered with them. Reporters were devoured before the viewing public. The faces of the zombies would forever be engrained in the minds of those of us "lucky" enough to still be alive. Ratted clothes. Bones sticking out of flesh. Rotting faces crusted with the blood of their victims. The worst were the ones whose skin had disintegrated around their mouths, leaving an eternal, deathly scowl. I'll never forget those scowls.

I hadn't left the closet I barricaded myself in since They first broke into my apartment. I only slept a few hours. Sleep left you too vulnerable. I didn't want to go that way. If I was going to be killed by those undead sons of bitches, I was going to go out fighting. My dad would have wanted that.

I had no idea if my family was still alive. There was no communication left. Phones, internet, TV--those things belonged in the past. I was reduced to drinking my own piss and eating the roaches that scampered around me. Sometimes I'd get lucky and kill a rat. I began to think that death would be better than life. At least there was food, water, beds, and peace in Heaven.

I lost count of the days since I'd been locked away in my prison. My whole body was a mass of agony. I was dizzy, and I constantly saw spots. My fingers and toes were numb. My stomach hurt. My lips were cracked and bleeding, while every breath I took felt like a knife digging into my heart.

I couldn't go on like this anymore. I had developed a dry heaving cough that ripped my throat apart and made it feel like it was on fire. I was starving. Dehydrated. I started to see things and hear things. I was going crazy. This wasn't living.

Slowly, I grabbed the doorknob and pulled myself up. My legs were shaking and it took me several minutes to find my balance. Leaning against the door, I closed my eyes and took several deep breaths. If there was anything in my stomach I would have thrown up, but I'd eaten my supply of roaches two days ago. I think…

"Okay, Monica," I coached myself in a whispery voice. "You can do this."

Taking a deep breath, I prepared myself for whatever was waiting for me out there.

Carefully, I opened the door and stepped out into the blinding light that poured through my apartment's blinds. Grimacing, I shielded my eyes and blinked several times. A few rogue tears formed at the corners of my eyes.

The first thing I noticed when I stepped outside was the smell. The odor of death assaulted my nostrils and caused me to fall back against the door with a groan.

The door to my apartment had been ripped off the hinges and thrown against my couch. A pair of children's sneakers was lying outside in the hall. My next door neighbor had a little boy. I wondered if they were his. I couldn't bring myself to go outside and see if they were attached to a body.

Standing there for a long moment, I listened. It was quiet. Too quiet. I felt a million goose pimples sprout along my arms like unwanted weeds. Hollywood was never quiet. I didn't like it. I cautiously made my way through the apartment toward the window, which overlooked Hollywood Hills. I had to look outside one last time. I had to see if anything was left, if anyone else was alive.

Glass crunched beneath my sneakers. Sticking my head out of the window, I nearly had a heart attack. My neighborhood looked like a war zone. Dried blood and bits of flesh coated the other buildings and the sidewalk. Most of the windows had been smashed, and smoke from several small fires curled sensuously up towards the sky.

"Jesus," I whispered.

A low, hungry growl caused me to jump. Slowly, I turned around. Something that was once a man had been watching me, its hateful eyes glaring at me like a cobra sizing up its prey. Its clothes were tattered and trailed behind like tentacles, and its skin looked like old dried leather and was cracked and peeling in several places. What little hair it did have was tangled and knotted.

"Hungry?" I asked, staring right back at it. The thing growled in response. "Well fuck you," I continued defiantly. "You're not gonna eat me alive."

Closing my eyes, I felt myself fall backwards out of the window. I held my breath and wondered if I would feel the impact when I hit the ground...

I don't know how long I was unconscious. When I slowly began to come around, the first thing I noticed was that I was looking into the face of an elderly woman. Her long, smoky gray hair was pinned up in a loose bun. Her wrinkled face was smeared with dirt and her clothes stank of dried sweat. My head and back were killing me. A weak moan spilled over my lips and it hurt like a mother.

"She's comin' 'round," the elderly woman called to some unknown persons in a heavy southern accent.

"Are you an angel?" I croaked out weakly.

"No, honey. I ain't no angel. I stock the produce at Ralph's."

"Am I in Heaven?"

"No darlin'. You're still in California. Hell, we saw you fall from that window while we were gettin' supplies," she explained.

"Supplies?" I asked, not comprehending.

"Food. Blankets. Don't know how much longer we can keep goin' into the city through with those sons of bitches down there. There's more and more of those damn things."

"Die, you zombie bastards!" a raspy voice behind me suddenly exclaimed, making me jump. Seconds later, I heard a hail of gunfire.

"Step on it, Jimmy!" the woman yelled. "They're gainin' on us."

"Where are we going?" I asked. I was sure this was some kind of death hallucination. Maybe I was in Purgatory.

"The Hills. A bunch of us are holed up in a cave up there. Hope you like rattlesnake and mountain lion. Those are the only animals that aren't infected."

"I've been living on piss and roaches," I answered. "I'm not expecting fine dining."

The woman smiled and lovingly caressed my cheek. I wondered if she'd been a grandmother. Nurturing seemed to be second-nature to her.

"You look familiar," the raspy voice said as he continued to fire at them.

"You probably saw me on TV. I am…was...an actress," I answered, suddenly feeling sad as I remembered my old life.

"No kidding," the man said. "What's your name?"

"Monica Saint John."

"No kidding," he whistled, impressed. "What an honor. You were my favorite actress. I rubbed one out a few times while looking at your picture…"

"Frank!" the woman scolded him. "You should be ashamed."

"It's okay," I half laughed, half coughed. "I'm flattered."

"See, Evelyn. She's flattered. I loved that zombie series you were in."

"Thanks," I responded with a weak smile.

"Ironic," he chuckled. "It's almost like we're in an episode of that series."

"Frank, no one wants to talk about zombies right now," Evelyn scolded.

"Jimmy, use that lead foot. I'm outta ammo," Frank yelled ignoring Evelyn.

"This thing doesn't go any faster," the one called Jimmy shouted back.

We drove for what felt like hours into the Hills. The sun was high above us and beat down without mercy. Buzzards, lured by the smell of death, were the only animals around, and they circled us ominously. It was too quiet and I hated it.

Finally, we stopped.

"Let's get her into the cave," the old woman said.

Frank scooped me up and carried me into the musky, cool cave. I could hear the sound of dripping water and it smelled of mold.

We went deeper and deeper into the cave. It felt like we walked all the way to Chicago.

When we got to the back I stared around, wide eyed. It was like a little city. There were dozens of men, women and children. Blankets were on the ground. Everyone was dirty, and a few were eating out of cracked dishes like Neanderthals, never taking their eyes off me as they scooped up their food with their hands. I understood what it felt like to be a refugee.

"Jesus…" I sighed.

"We found another one," Frank said. "Monica Saint John. The famous TV actress."

"They're coming!" a teenage voice yelled from the cave's entrance. It echoed off the walls.

A young boy, no older than fifteen, ran toward us. His feet were bare and stained with dirt.

"They're coming. About fifty of 'em. They're heading right towards us," he panted, out of breath.

We all turned towards the entrance. The darkness would have rendered our attackers nearly invisible, and in that tense silence, the anticipation was unbearable.

We could hear their low growls. We could hear their nails scratching at the cave walls.

"Is there another way out?" I asked, looking around the cave in vain.

Their eyes were the only answer I needed. It was the same look I had seen on the news when people were attacked and knew they were going to die.

Hopelessness.

DAUGHTER OF THE DEAD

TIMOTHY TARKELLY

It's sad to think about life before my few friends lost their souls. There was a time when life was simple. People were just people. I used to have hobbies and ambitions. No matter how I would spend my time, it was mine.

For instance, I would go to the movies by myself a lot. Not that I mind. I mean, movies aren't any better or worse if people are with you. Regardless, after the movie was over, I would always feel like a loser. I think even a girl like me could find someone to go to the movies with. My friend, Miranda, would come with me a couple of times, but she was simply too annoying.

Nothing ever made sense to her and I had to explain every word the characters said. Also, she always complains about the kinds of movies I like. Honestly, I think horror films are the only way to get your money out of the cinema experience. A good scary movie can drive you to laughter, shock, and fear and I like going beyond that. Why would anyone pay twelve bucks to cry?

Besides, movies are pretty much the only attraction Loisburg has to offer its youth. There are always a hundred kids my age crowded outside of the theater. Most of them go to school with me. Basically, all of them look directly at me when I walk by and pretend not to remember who I am.

One evening after a movie, and not quite ready to begin my walk home, I stood at the edge of the sidewalk and watched the teenagers mix and mingle while they waited for their rides. Almost instantly, I saw the man I adored, standing amongst a sea of people who were hardly worth his company.

Nathan was the most beautiful person I'd ever seen in my life. He wasn't over-muscled, extremely tall, or any of that uber-manly gross stuff. He was simply...beautiful. I was full on staring, my eyes fighting between his perfectly unkempt auburn hair and his piercing blue eyes, when Brad interrupted my fantasy.

"Hey, Julie. What're you doing?" Brad asked, looking up at me. He had to be a foot shorter than I was.

I thought about telling him that I was making a list of all the things I would do to Nathan, but that would probably just make him cry.

"Nothing, Brad. Leave me alone. Haven't you learned your lesson?" A week before that evening, I got suspended for fighting with Brad, although it wasn't much of a fight. He kept looking at my chest, so I slapped him. The poor little guy. He went straight to the floor, and I'm pretty sure he cried. If he hadn't have been such a baby, I wouldn't have had to suffer an in-school suspension.

"No, I know you didn't mean to hurt me. Anyway, what're you up to?" Brad didn't give up. He maintained a long-time infatuation with me that I never understood.

"I'm waiting for my dad to come pick me up," I lied.

"How's your dad?" Brad asked. The question kind of struck a nerve and I immediately wanted the conversation to be over.

"Good," I replied. "Why do you care?"

"Well, my dad said he hasn't seen him in a while at the restaurant."

Brad's father was Officer Quentin Holting. He was the chief of the Loisburg Police Department and somewhat of a local hero. At least, he was treated like one. He would go to my father's restaurant every morning for a free breakfast. He was also a widow, his wife passing away of cancer two years ago.

"Yeah," I said. "I don't know what his deal is."

"Oh, well...if you ever need someone to talk to..."

I laughed in his face. "Thanks anyway, Brad." I snorted.

"Right," Brad's face grew bright red. "Anyway, do you want to ride home with me and my dad? I'm sure he won't mind."

My laughing slowly subsided. "That's all right. My ride should be here soon."

"Okay. See you at school tomorrow." He shrugged and turned to walk away. His little frame was sulking across the parking lot. I actually did feel bad for him.

"Hey, Brad!" I called after him.

"Yeah?"

"Thanks anyway." He smiled and went on, walking towards his father's patrol car.

As soon as they were out of sight, I started walking. The entire way home, I tried to make sense out of the way my dad had been acting lately. He hadn't talked in a week. When I got in trouble for slapping Brad, I didn't get a lecture. I didn't get anything. I kind of thought it was a disappointed father-silent treatment sort of thing. I'm pretty sure he'd stopped bathing altogether. My house had started reeking something awful.

I barely noticed until I ate dinner with him one evening. He would just stare down at his food and he smelled like death. What I had assumed was sweat had pooled around his hairline and slowly dripped onto the table. I wanted to choke myself from breathing that stench in. I shouldn't call it sweat. It's more like the condensation that builds inside of the crisper when you let the vegetables rot.

After I got home from the movies that night, it all came to-gether.

He was standing in the doorway between the kitchen and the living room. Water dripped from his body and pooled onto the floor as if he'd been rained on or showered without taking off his clothes. As soon as I realized that it wasn't water, but rather the sweat I once saw at the dinner table, I immediately ran to my room and came to the conclusion that my dad was a zombie. Maybe it was from all those horror movies I'd watched, or maybe I was the one who was crazy.

I said the word out loud and felt really stupid for thinking such a ridiculous thing. But then I replayed everything my dad had done in my head. If that wasn't it, then what was his deal? I sat on my bed, thinking about reality and its lack of undead creatures, but my imagination was getting the best of me. I was suddenly very glad my little sister decided to stay with mom, who lived a couple of towns over. She was sensitive to a father who ignored her, and besides, he was getting creepier by the day.

Finally, I negotiated with myself.

"Better safe than sorry," I said aloud and began shuffling my dresser across the carpet. I pressed it as tightly as I could against my bedroom door. Looking at my homemade barricade, I knew at once that I was going to have to move it right back. I felt like an idiot. I put on some sweats and went to sleep, putting off the dresser until morning.

I awoke with a jump. Instinctively, I looked at the alarm clock to discover it was just after six o'clock in the morning. I closed my eyes and tried to fall back to sleep. Then, I heard what must have woken me up in the first place.

My door knob was rattling.

"Dad?" I asked and the noise stopped.

I suddenly remembered the night before, and the sweat and stench from my zombie father. Panic quickly ensued.

"Dad?" I said again, almost yelling this time.

Instead of answering, he started on the door again, gradually increasing the severity of his knocking until he was pounding on it. Suddenly, he slammed into it and the dresser lurched forward an inch. I immediately rolled to the floor and felt under my bed for the first pair of sneakers I could find. Within seconds, I was out the window and running down the alley as fast as I could. When I reached the end of the street, I stopped and thought about my situation.

There was a ridiculously good chance I was overreacting. Regardless, my father had just scared me far too much to just go back home. I decided to go to the Quick-Mart across the street from the high school and wait for the morning bell to ring.

I didn't have to wait long and soon it was time to go to school. I needed someone to talk to, so I waited outside of Miranda's homeroom class, hoping she would be there before the bell rang, or at all. She hadn't been to school for nearly a week. As I leaned against the door, handsome Nathan Rosenthal appeared from around the corner.

Nathan's attire always surprised me. I'd never met a high school boy with such great taste. His mother or sister must pick out his clothes for him. I was tracing the outline of his body underneath his clothing with my eyes when he started talking to me.

"Hey, Julie."

I'd never heard him say my name before.

"Yep! That's me." I could barely talk. A sudden assessment of the clothes I was wearing left me even more breathless. In my haste to escape my house, I hadn't bothered to change out of my pajamas, and the sneakers I'd chosen made my feet look *huge*.

"Were you just staring at me? Are you okay?"

My face was filling with as much red as it could manage.

I stammered. "No, I, uh, must have zoned out or something. It's kind of early, you know?"

"Right." He smiled at me and for a moment, all of my problems vanished. "Well, see you in class."

"Yeah." I nodded like a bobblehead and Nathan walked away with a grin. My problems hadn't vanished at all. They'd just gotten a lot worse.

Regardless of how embarrassed I was, I was a little excited that he'd mentioned seeing me in class. I didn't know if it meant he was going to talk to me more or if he was literally going to see me. Maybe 'seeing me' meant he'd be looking at me. I flattered myself with the idea.

I gave up on Miranda and went to class. It wasn't even eight in the morning and I'd already abandoned my house out of fear that my dad was a zombie and made an ass of myself in front of Nathan. I wasn't going to explain my home troubles and have Miranda tell me I was crazy, too. My wild imagination attacked me with a million different questions, all jumbled together.

How could my father be a zombie? It was impossible? But if he wasn't, then what was wrong with him? Did Nathan actually like me? Where was Miranda?

My first period class, as well as the others, seemed to go by in seconds. My mind was so completely scatterbrained, jumping from one horrendous scenario to another, that I couldn't recall walking between classes after each bell rang.

Fourth period was different, however. Nathan was in my fourth period class. Even after leaving my house at six in the morning to escape my father's violent episode, the only thing I cared about when I walked into Senior English was Nathan 'seeing' me. And he did exactly that. He waved and I blushed.

"You awake yet?"

"Huh?" I almost snarled at him, completely unable to control the volume of my voice.

"You were tired this morning, remember?"

"Oh, yeah. Sorry. I feel a lot better."

He shook his head and I hurried to my seat. I couldn't remember the last time I had a conversation with Nathan, but I'd just had two in one day. Granted, they weren't very successful. Either way, I was positively beaming when the intercom sounded.

"Julie Cassentino to the office," the voice over the loud speaker said, garbled with a hint of static. "Julie Cassentino, please come to the office." There was a pause, as if the voice wasn't sure if it should say the next part, then, "You're father is here."

I stopped breathing when the voice mentioned my dad. Goosebumps ran along my arms and I wanted to cower under the desk.

"Hey, Julie," a soothing voice said over my shoulder.

I turned to see Nathan smiling at me. "You better get going."

"Right," I blushed yet again and darted out of the classroom with a nod to the teacher.

At first, knowing my father was in the school scared me to no end. It occurred to me that maybe it had been an intruder the previous night, and after realizing I was missing with my door caved in and my window open, my dad had come to school to see if I was here, and when finding out I was, he wanted to check on me. My spirits were lifting and I was practically sprinting to the office.

I was stopped by my school counselor.

"Julie, hold on a second," Mr. Bolan said from somewhere under his untrimmed mustache.

I stopped in my tracks, confused, and for the first time that day, fully alert.

"Is your father okay?"

"Uh, yeah. I guess so." I wondered if he could tell I was lying.

"Well, he's..." Mr. Bolan looked at me with an almost fatherly expression. I could tell he was deeply concerned. "You know, he didn't even talk when he came in here."

"What do you mean?" I was trembling.

"He just sort of...walked in. One of the secretaries recognized him as your father. He won't respond to a thing we ask him."

I looked at him in silence, then he continued.

"Look, Julie. I don't mean to pry, but what's going on with him? He seems to have an...odor."

I nearly choked as I said, "Everything's fine, Mr. Bolan." I was almost in tears. I wanted to tell him what was going on, and what my theories were, but I couldn't see that making things any better for me. I abruptly walked away from him, and as soon as I rounded the corner of the hall, I sprinted for the front doors. I needed to get out of there.

My head was spinning in thirteen different directions. It wasn't until I made it a few blocks from the school that I realized I was headed towards my house. The realization made me stop for a second. It was the only place I would run into my dad again. I kept running anyway.

It made the most sense. That way, I could at least grab some of my stuff and maybe use the phone to call my mom for help. I don't know how many times I tried to convince my parents that I needed a cell phone. In our small town, cell phones were just catching on amongst teens as 'must have' items, and more than any other time, I really needed one.

I completely skipped the front door and ran around the house to my window. It took me a couple of tries, but I hopped up and over the windowsill and landed roughly on my bedroom floor. Wasting no time, I emptied the contents of my backpack onto the carpet and filled it with clothes. Then, I took another bag to the kitchen and filled it with a random assortment of potato chips and bottled water.

For the first time in what felt like forever, I took a moment to rest. What was once my house, humble, but safe, was going to be dead to me. I prayed that whatever happened would be temporary. Tears started welling up, squeezing their way between my eyelids. Was I making the right choice in leaving? Frankly, I didn't know what else to do and I had to do something.

That was when I committed the most sentimental act of my life. I snatched the family pictures off the mantle and forced them into my backpack. I held the last photo in my hand for a moment, studying the glimpse from my not-so-distant history. The picture was just over a year old, taken right before my parents' divorce. My mom looked pretty as always, her slender body's radiance engulfing my sister and I. Liza's hair was a mess, but in the cutest way possible, and I suppose even I looked pretty in the picture. My hair looked way more blonde than it should have, due to the sunlight, but the angle was just right. My smile was timed perfectly, and I could see that I was beginning to look like my mother. I should be so lucky.

I remembered I needed to call her and started walking towards the phone. I jumped when there came a banging on the front door.

My breath escaped me. I somehow fought through the urge to faint and turned towards the hallway, making a break for my bedroom. I couldn't have been more than three feet away from the window when I heard a noise coming from outside. Without even thinking about it, I dropped to the floor and rolled against the wall, underneath the window. I covered my mouth with a hand, trying to keep my sobbing as quiet as possible.

I could hear someone stumbling in the yard, then a grunt, and before I could make sense of it, a hand emerged through the window and grabbed onto the window frame. My hands covered my eyes, and I let out a cry. I couldn't handle what was happening. It was father! He'd come back to get me!

The figure had entered my room and was kneeling over me. The urge to faint came rushing back, then I heard a voice, one I recognized immediately.

"Julie, you're okay! It's me, Officer Holting."

My entire body relaxed at once, but I still didn't want to open my eyes.

"Come on, upsa-daisy. We gotta go, now," he said.

I was more confused than before. There had been too many incidents like this today. I didn't want to expend the energy to speak. Instead, I ran and grabbed the bags I'd packed and then we were out the door and in his squad car. Brad, my eternal admirer, was waiting for us in the back seat.

"Do you know what's going on, Julie?" Officer Holting asked. I shook my head. His tone was calm and concerned. I immediately felt safer than I had all day.

"Well," he continued, "Bolan called me and said you ran away from the school, and then he told me about your father's...behavior."

"Where is he?" I asked.

"He's at the hospital." Officer Holting's voice trailed off.

"I don't understand," I admitted.

He took a deep breath, as if he were sorting his thoughts and choosing his words carefully. "He attacked me, Julie."

I gasped, and grabbed onto his arm. "Are you okay?"

"I'm fine. He...I detained him. When I put the cuffs on him..." He took a moment and I waited for him to speak. I didn't want to make it any more difficult for him. "When I put the cuffs on him, all of the skin under them slid off."

"What do you mean?" I asked, almost in a whisper.

"Well, it's like his skin *was* completely rotted. Actually, his skin was completely rotted. He's in a clean room at the hospital. The doctors say he's the fourth person today to be admitted under the same circumstances. That Miranda Ports girl and her parents came in a few days earlier."

That was another piece to suddenly fit into the puzzle.

"Is it some kind of disease, or something?" I asked.

"That's a very good question. Honestly, I don't think the doctors are gonna have an answer any time soon. The CDC is sending a team out. The State is sending some people out, too."

"To look at my dad?" I asked, utterly confused.

"No. I mean, yes. But they'll be coming to shut down the local water supply... stuff like that."

Brad said, "So, the water has some kind of disease in it that makes your skin rot?"

"Not exactly," Officer Holting explained. "Personally, I don't think the water has anything to do with it. There'd be a lot more people affected if that were the case. All of us seem to be fine, but where else could they start?"

None of us had any ideas. The car was silent for a few moments. Brad reached from the back and put his hand on my shoulder. The small contact was enough to make me start crying again.

"Officer Holting?" I began.

"Call me Quentin," he replied.

"Is that all that's wrong with my father?"

His expression softened. He breathed deeply and his brow furrowed. "Julie...you father didn't have a pulse. It's almost like he's..." He didn't finish his sentence.

Of course, he didn't have to. I grabbed Brad's hand, as he awkwardly sat halfway on his seat, just so he could offer me a small token of comfort. My mind radiated with pain. I was simply too overwhelmed. The thought of more people like my father suffering from the same affliction scared me. There were more people turning into whatever he was.

Fifteen minutes later, we pulled into the police station parking lot and Quentin sent Brad and I into his office. I immediately tried calling my mother, but received no answer. It was only a little after four and she was probably on her way home after picking up Liza. My mom had a cell phone, but I couldn't remember the number. I rarely called it. It was, however, posted on the fridge at my house.

I slumped into the big leather chair behind the desk, while Brad walked around the office, poking at the trinkets and awards that decorated the room. As my exhaustion suddenly overwhelmed me, I drifted off to sleep.

My eyes snapped open as Quentin shook me.

"Julie, we have to go, now!"

I was still half asleep. Although I didn't really register what he said, I followed him outside anyway, rubbing my eyes the entire time. We were apparently taking Quentin's SUV. Brad waited for us patiently while he held bags of clothes over his face in an attempt to hide his red-rimmed eyes. I could tell he'd been crying. We all climbed in and were soon on our way.

Through all the chaos, my mind was still trying to shut down and rest, and when the SUV came to a sudden halt, my brain sort of clicked. Directly in front of the vehicle was a man with the same affliction as my father. Half of his body lacked flesh, and exposed muscle shone wetly in the sun. He glared menacingly at us with bright yellow eyes. I screamed louder than I ever had before.

Quentin floored it, running the man down. A mixture of blood, bile, and gore found its way all over the windshield and front grille. I would have puked if I hadn't been screaming so hard.

"Stay away from the windows, guys," Quentin said, somehow still maintaining a sense of calm.

I unlatched my seat belt and crawled into the back seat with Brad. He pulled me to the floorboards and we closed our eyes, scrunched into an awkward ball. I tried not to think of the visuals that corresponded with the noises I could hear. A series of thuds echoed their way all along the exterior of the SUV and random grunts and shrill calls followed every bump.

"What the hell is going on?" I finally asked.

"They're zombies," Brad said, as if it was the most normal thing in the world.

"Bullshit, that's impossible," I replied, knowing full well that what he was saying was true.

"No, I'm telling the truth. A lot more people went to the hospital today. Dad went down to check what was going on and when he was there, he said the main doors burst open and all of these zombies came charging out of there."

The noises seemed to let up at once and what had been chaos was replaced with the constant whirring of tires on concrete. Brad and I sat up in the back seat. A glance through the side window verified that we were on the highway.

"Julie?" Quentin spoke up. "Your mother lives in Hallsboro, right?"

"Yeah."

"Would she mind some visitors for a while?"

I didn't have to ask why he was willing to abandon the town that he swore to protect. I figured it was because of his son. Brad was all he had left and family came first, even before his oath to protect the town. I was a kid, not a parent: who was I to judge?

When we pulled up to my mother's house, I was immediately disheartened when I saw that all the lights were off. I led Brad and Quentin around back, because she never locked the back door. It was something my dad used to always yell at her about.

Regardless of her absence, I was still relieved to be there. I was at least forty miles away from the zombies that were terrorizing Loisburg.

As we entered the house with me in the lead, a sudden realization caused me to erupt into another shrill scream.

"Oh God, we have to go back!" I shouted and started pulling at Brad and Quentin.

"Hold on, Julie," Quentin said, trying to calm me down. "What are you talking about?"

"My mom. My sister. This was our night to have dinner together at my house!" With everything that had happened, I'd completely forgotten what day it was.

Quentin's face melted into a look of either disgust or supreme irritation.

"You're saying they're back in Loisburg?" Brad asked as he ran his fingers through his hair. He already knew the answer. He shook his head and couldn't hold his frustration in check. "Why didn't you say something before now? Don't you realize that we could have died on our way here? We can't go back there!"

"Hold on a second, son," Quentin muttered as he sat down on the couch. "By now the National Guard and State Police should have been alerted and are en route. Honestly, they'll probably get there faster than us even if we leave right now."

He was doing his best to reason with me, but I melted to the floor. I was utterly horrified by the possibilities of what could happen between that very moment and whenever help arrived in Loisburg. We were safe in my mother's house, so far away from the madness. If I were Quentin, there would have been no way that I would have given that up. Brad, however, saw the desperation in my eyes and gave his father the same sad look. He sighed and finally said, "Dad?"

"Yeah, okay," Quentin nodded. "Let's go."

We left, preparing ourselves once again for the creatures that crowded the streets of Loisburg. Our plan was to go directly to my house. On the way, Quentin let me use his cell phone to call my mom's cell but it went right to voice mail. I had to get in touch with her. Was she safe or was she even now trapped by more of those creatures?

There was a small, military roadblock set up five miles outside the Loisburg city limits. Just like Quentin had said the National Guard had arrived.

Quentin had me reach into the glove box to retrieve his information, and I was very surprised to find two handguns lying on top of the papers. One of them was a small revolver. The other was massive pistol; the kind of gun that heroes always used in the movies.

When we came to a stop, I was very surprised to see the soldiers pointing weapons at us. One approached the driver's side door to talk to Quentin.

"You can't pass through, the town's under quarantine," the soldier barked.

"Look, I'm the Police Chief of Loisburg."

"Don't care, you can't pass through," the soldier repeated.

"Well, did you guys retrieve anyone from town?"

"No, sir. We have strict orders to maintain quarantine until further notice."

Quentin grew impatient. "Are you going to shoot me if I drive through anyway?"

"Well, no, but the next roadblock will when I call ahead."

"The next one?" Quentin asked.

"Yeah, a real one. They set us up out here to stop people from going further, but only to warn. Their orders are to keep anything and anyone from getting out of town. If you don't cooperate with them, they'll take you into custody...or shoot you if you resist."

I shuddered when the soldier said 'anything.'

Quentin swallowed the insult and put the SUV into drive. He exchanged impatient looks with the soldier, who finally waved his men out of our way to let us continue down the road.

"Julie, there's no way we're getting into Loisburg," Quentin told me.

"But we have to."

When we had driven one mile, evidence of the 'real' roadblock came into view and Quentin pulled over and stopped. Spotlights were posted twenty feet high, and military vehicles were arranged to completely block access to the road.

"Is there another way we can go?" I asked Quentin.

"Well, even if there was, it would be guarded the same."

I turned around to look at Brad and he gave me a weak smile. It hadn't really occurred to me until then that Brad had been an important person through this whole mess. I smiled back at him, already feeling guilty for what I was going to do next.

The SUV slowed, then stopped when the roadblock was in full view. I opened the glove box and retrieved the two pistols.

"Hey, don't touch those," Quentin warned me, and before he could do anything, I opened the door and sprinted for the treeline. I could hear him yelling after me, and I hoped he wouldn't try to follow. To be honest, I felt horrible. The Holtings had been nothing but helpful. They had taken me all the way back to town, despite putting themselves in danger for me. Instead of repaying them, I'd just made their problems worse. But I wasn't going to let my mother and sister stay trapped inside of that town. I didn't give it much thought about how crazy what I was doing truly was. After all, what could I really do to help them?

So I ran, in spite of my weary body's misery and my lungs' inability to breathe. The small revolver was tucked into my back pocket and I held the large pistol in my right hand.

Once I reached the other side of the treeline, I could tell I only had a quarter mile or so to go before I got to a small patch of farmland and into the town of Loisburg.

Sucking in a deep breath and letting it out, I began to run again.

When I finally reached the edge of town, I don't think anything could have prepared me for what I saw.

An amber glow from the setting sun revealed streets filled with zombies. I choked back a scream of fear that I would been seen, and placed my hand over my mouth. My hometown had been invaded, but I couldn't turn back. My family needed me.

I continued running, trying my hardest to stay out of sight, until I was able to make a direct line to my house. Without a moment's hesitation I went for it. I darted down the street and took a right. My house was only a few blocks away. I took a left and immediately wished I hadn't.

There were three of them standing in the street before me, two men and a woman. I really didn't know what to do. Aside from my father's lashing out at me, I hadn't seen any proof of violent behavior. One of the men opened his mouth and let out a horrendous snarl.

I got scared and decided to shoot him anyway, not wanting to be attacked. When I squeezed the trigger on the pistol, nothing happened, so I searched the gun for a safety. I didn't know where it was but quickly found a small lever on the left side. I flicked it and tried again, holding it in a two-handed grip. My eyes were squeezed shut as I fired.

The heavy gun whipped my hands back over my head when I fired it and the explosive report rang in my ears. When I opened my eyes, I saw that the zombie was on the ground, its left leg crumbled beneath it. I fired again, aiming a little higher, and watched its head explode in a cloud of brain and skull chunks. I did the same to the next one, trying to keep the gun under better control. By the third, I took off the head with one shot. I realized that I had no extra ammunition and I hoped I didn't run into too many more of them. I'd just shot three people, but at that moment in time, I wasn't even fazed. Maybe it was from playing too many video games or maybe I was in shock.

In front of my house, there were two more undead creatures. It took me four shots to bring them down. I had no idea if they were actually dead, but my method seemed to be working. To my right, I heard a scream. It was definitely human. I looked in time to see a man surrounded by zombies. They latched onto him and began biting him wherever they could. I watched in horror as the man went down with his throat torn out.

For a moment, silence ensued as the zombies fed, then the man rose to his feet, assuming the same terrifying posture as his predators. In a matter of moments, he'd become one of them, too. I dashed to my house, leaving a trail of tears behind me.

I stopped on the threshold upon seeing that the front door had been kicked in, the doorframe a mess of jagged splinters. Another member of the living dead stood in my living room.

I fired one shot that hit him in the chest, then followed with another for good measure, this one hitting him in the head right between the eyes. After the first shot, the gun made a hollow click. It was out of bullets. Before I could reach into my back pocket for the revolver, something struck me in the back of my head. I rolled to the floor. When I looked up, I immediately recognized my attacker.

The red cardigan he was wearing was covered in blood, mucus, and a smattering of other bodily fluids. His hair was no longer perfect; large clumps had been pulled out to expose a pale scalp. The once perfect jawline was broken and hanging limply as he swung his bloody head back and forth.

Nathan had not only become one of them, he was trying to kill me.

I reached for the revolver again and my fingertips glanced along the cold metal grip, then I had it within my grasp, but the undead version of Nathan picked me up by my legs, and the gun slipped away. I beat my fists on him as hard as I could. For a second, he lost his balance and let me go. I landed on my shoulder and was momentarily too stunned to move. Pain writhed up and down my arm.

I could see the revolver was two feet away. The gun was within my reach.

At that moment, I needed it to be over. Nathan was the boy I'd wanted to kiss, the boy that made me blush, and now I was about to blow his head off.

My former crush looked at me with tainted, dead eyes, then opened his mouth to show blood-soaked teeth. He'd fed already by the looks of it.

I aimed the gun at his face, and with my eyes closed, squeezed the trigger.

Even after I blew his head off, I kept firing until I heard the dry click of an empty chamber. I didn't realize that my eyes were closed until the tears began to flow freely.

But there was no time to feel useless, and there was no telling how many more of them would come into my house. I ran into the kitchen and picked up the phone, then called my mother's cell again, hoping for the best.

Honestly, I expected it to be a lost cause. When she answered, I experienced a feeling of relief unparalleled by any emotion I'd felt before.

"Julie?" my mother said from the other end.

"Mom! Oh, my God. Is Liza with you? Are you okay?"

"She's here. We're in the high school," she assured me.

"What are you doing there?"

"Mr. Bolan called me...look, we need to get out of here."

"Officer Holting is waiting for me on the other side of the roadblock. Do you guys have a car?"

She stopped to whisper with someone else, likely Mr. Bolan.

"Yes, we do. Mark's car is in the parking lot, but we're not sure we can make it."

"Mark?" I asked. I began to draw assumptions about her relationship with Mr. Bolan. I assumed it extended farther than a concerned faculty member consulting with a parent. "Does he have Officer Holting's phone number?"

More whispering.

"Yes we do, honey."

"Call him and, tell him where you are. I'm coming to get you."

"No, honey, that's crazy, you can't. You need to..."

I hung up the phone to evade an emotional exchange and her protests.

There was a shotgun in my father's closet, and luckily there was an entire box of shells on the top shelf. I'd gone on a handful of hunting trips with him in the past to amuse him.

Maybe my dad had wanted a boy but had gotten me and Liza instead. I'd never hit anything, but he'd let me fire his shotgun a few times, and he'd taught me how to load it.

I needed a minute to figure out how to remember how to load it, but it soon came back to me. I took out his hunting vest from the closet and filled every compartment with shells, then stuffed my jean pockets with more.

It was time to take on an army of animated corpses that inhabited the six blocks between me and my high school.

Minutes later, I was outside and walking down the street.

When I turned the first corner, there were too many to count before me, so I chose my victims carefully and fired as I ran through them.

My focus was only on the ones that were close enough to hurt me. Every once in a while, the recoil of the shotgun would twist my arms around and make the pain in my shoulder grow even stronger. I kept running anyway, only pausing to reload when necessary.

My frantic run seemed surreal. I certainly wasn't any kind of a soldier, but none of that mattered when everything that was important to me was being threatened. Adrenaline was a wonderful thing.

By running and shooting, I made it a few more blocks, and when I was only two blocks away from the high school, I ran out of ammunition.

I tried holding onto the barrel and wielding it like a bat, but it was so hot from the continuous firing that it burned my hands, not that I had the strength to do much damage this way either.

I held the shotgun in front of me and sprinted though a crowd of zombies. Weaving between them, I ran until I was half a block away from the high school.

Suddenly, I found myself surrounded by more than a dozen animated corpses. I remembered the man that had been devoured, only to transform moments later as one of the walking dead. I knew I didn't want that fate to happen to me.

Their eager hands reached for me, and I knew that I couldn't panic. There had to be a way through them. I recognized many of the faces. All the parents and friends of people I went to school with wanted to eat me.

The shotgun was snatched out of my hands, and before I could adjust my stance to protect myself, a barrage of bloody fists rained down upon me. I threw my arms over my head and screamed for my mother as I was forced to the ground.

I'd failed. My mother and sister were still in the school and would never know what happened to me. Quentin and Brad were probably being detained by the National Guard. And me...my soul was about to evaporate as I became one of the walking dead.

I was about to accept my fate when a loud crack, followed by a thud, provided a comforting sense of relief. I heard it again and then again.

Bodies fell around me, headless, while others turned to the source of gunfire. After a few more moments, I found myself lying on the pavement, unharmed, and no 'living' zombies in sight.

"Julie!" Quentin shouted.

I slowly stood up, and Quentin ran towards me.

"Are you all right?" he asked me, offering his arm for support to steady me.

"Yeah, how'd you get here?"

"I took a back road to old man Benton's property. Drove through a few corn fields..."

"Good thing you drive an SUV," I said.

He offered a forced chuckle and started walking me to the SUV. "I shouldn't have left the town," Quentin said. "I was supposed to protect them, but instead I ran, only thinking of protecting Brad."

I didn't have the strength to reassure him. I had taken a few blows to the head, and I felt dizzy. I leaned into him heavily. "My mom's in the school," I said, drifting out of consciousness.

"Actually, she's in my SUV. Brad got her and your sister while I saved you."

I was consumed with relief. As my strength waned, Quentin had to carry me the rest of the way.

Mom was in the passenger seat and Liza and Mark Bolan were in the back seat of the SUV with Brad. Quentin opened the rear door and I crawled in to fit behind the seats.

I probably had a mild concussion, because though I should have told my family I was glad to see them and that I loved them, I simply laid my head down and passed out.

When I awoke, I was sore from head to toe. I was sleeping on a cot and had no idea where I was.

"Mom?" I said quietly.

A soldier poked his head through a fissure of light. I was in a tent.

"Good, you're up," he said. "They're waiting for you."

"How long have I been out?"

"Only a couple of hours."

He led me to the SUV. The back was now filled with extra cans of gasoline and boxes of canned food.

The same soldier who was a jerk to us at the roadblock was talking to Quentin. "When you guys leave here, you're to go directly north to the state border. You'll be stopped by another barricade when you get there, just mention my name and they'll let you through."

"What about Hallsboro?" my mother asked.

"Overtaken," he replied coldly.

The expression on everyone's face was one of concern.

"I mean it, go straight north," the soldier said. "I'm gonna call every roadblock from here to there and tell them that if they see your SUV to let you through, that you're on a special mission for my Captain," the soldier half-smiled.

Quentin nodded and we all crammed into the seats, since the back was full of supplies. Liza sat on my lap and I squeezed her as tight as I could.

"Everyone ready?" Quentin asked the group and received a slew of unsure nods in return. I studied everyone's face and saw a mixture of exhaustion and terror. I must have looked the same.

Those feelings began to disappear as soon as we hit the highway and headed north, where the people were still people.

"So, Quentin," I said. "What did you give that soldier back there to get him to help us like that?"

Behind the steering wheel, Quentin shrugged his shoulders. "I gave him money."

"Really, how much?" I asked.

Quentin smiled. "About fifty thousand dollars."

The mouths of everyone in the SUV fell open.

Quentin laughed when he saw the looks on everyone's face. "Don't worry about it. I got the money from the evidence locker at the police station. It was from a bust over a year ago. We pulled over a van and found it was full of cash." His grin went from ear to ear. "The driver of the van was part of a counterfeiting ring. The money was fake."

I don't know whether it was the idea that the soldier had taken the bribe or the fact that the money was fake, but I found the idea to be hilarious. As I began to laugh, everyone joined in and soon we were all teary-eyed from laughter.

It was a good way to begin our journey.

FIGHTER'S BITE

WILLIAM TODD ROSE

The dented metal door muffled the roar of the crowd, but Bruno Swaggart could tell the house was packed. Drunk on moonshine, the audience banged aluminum chairs against the floor and the dull clangs echoed through the gymnasium like misfiring pistons. The erratic rhythm punctuated a cacophony of cat calls, shrill whistles, and a hundred voices vying for dominance in a sea of chaos.

Despite having weapons checked at the door, a few unruly spectators somehow managed to smuggle sidearms into the old school and the occasional gunshot rang out above the din. There were always a few in every crowd. Most didn't harbor any nefarious schemes-they were just good-old-boys who'd grown up embracing the concept that a party just wasn't a party unless there was gunplay involved.

At one point in his life, Bruno had thrived on the incomprehensible murmur of an expectant audience. It stirred something within him, working him into a frenzy in the same way that drums excited a tribal dancer.

Confidence would surge through his veins and he'd literally feel that anything was possible: he could punch through a brick wall with his bare hands and dance so quickly that his opponent would register nothing more than a blur. He was Superman, who had overcome his aversion to Kryptonite, an unstoppable juggernaut, two hundred and ten pounds of unleashed fury. But the Plague had changed all of that.

For the longest time, his greatest fight had been simply staying alive. There were even times when he'd considered taking a dive.

A well placed bullet to end the suffering, a knife pulled across the wrists-a sleep free from the nightmares which haunted his evenings: these all seemed like viable options in a world that no longer made sense.

Yet somehow Bruno found the strength to carry on. Now, with society struggling to emerge from the ashes of the old world like a crippled phoenix, he sat within the locker room of a burned-out high school and harbored no illusions. The boisterous crowd on the other side of the door hadn't paid dented cans of food and jugs of water to witness Bruno Swaggart participate in a sport he once loved-they came to see him die.

With his gloves laced tightly around un-taped fists, he leaned forward on the narrow bench and stared at cinder block walls that used to be red. The paint had peeled and chipped, revealing large swaths of gray block beneath. Flecks of crimson stuck in the pits and gouges, marring the surface of the masonry, and the contrast tricked Bruno's mind into creating order from chaos. His imagination formed pictures from these splotches of gray and red, but never anything as picturesque as the sun setting on a pristine beach or an unspoiled forest with trees striving to touch the stars. The patterns he saw within the flaking paint always became faces. They stared back at him with eyes as cold and unfeeling as the rusted pipes overhead, skin cracking and festering with hints of bone peeking through flesh twisted and disfigured by decay. They sneered through ravaged lips, revealing shattered teeth speckled with blood. Teeth which wanted nothing more than to bite and gnaw upon the flesh of the living…

From outside the locker room, Bruno heard the announcer's voice call out above the din of the crowd. The words were muddled and indistinct, but he knew the spiel well enough to understand the gist of it. Yelling through a megaphone like some 1950s era cheerleader, the announcer would string adjectives and adverbs into a rhythmic pitch designed to whip the already boisterous spectators into a fervor. They'd tasted blood by now. They'd been reduced to primal, savage beings that lusted after the spectacle that death could provide. Some of them pretended to pick favorites and held up cardboard signs with some fighter's name scrawled in crayon. Others dropped pretense, openly shouting "Kill 'em! Kill 'em!" without ever drawing a judgmental gaze from those around them. Deep down inside, they were all just as callous and bloodthirsty as those they'd come to watch.

Almost time now, the fighter thought.

Bruno hopped off the bench with a bounce. Taking several jabs at the air, he dropped into a slight crouch before hopping on the tips of his laced-up boots. Once, he would have had a small crew with him: a coach, a trainer, a medic…but the world had changed. He had changed, the sport had changed, everything had changed.

He simply didn't give a damn anymore.

Life was no longer about living, but staying alive. The bloodshed, the stench of rotting meat filling empty shops and streets. The images were forever burned into his mind and the nightmares they birthed-an echo of screams in corridors of memory: those things hardened him. Whether he lived or died was of no consequence. Everyone had to go sooner or later, and Bruno had no problem doing whatever it took to make sure his numbered days were as comfortable as possible.

Bowing his head, Bruno crossed himself and whispered his version of a prayer: "*Carpe diem.*" He slammed the metal door so hard it struck the wall with a clang and slapped his head with his gloves as he moved through a hallway lined with lockers. Just outside of the gymnasium's double doors, the tile was scorched, as if someone had once built a campfire there. The walls were decorated with graffiti, some messages strained for irony (*School's Out*) while others were as terse and stoic as a news report (*Salem's Dead. Stay Away*).

The roar of the crowd hit him like a body blow as the gym's doors were thrown open for him. It was as if the sound had pounced on the other side, just waiting for the two old men to do their job. A woman in a bikini strutted in front of the metal cage that dominated the basketball court. The left side of her face was scarred, a zigzagging chasm carved into flesh, and the tops of her thighs had the shiny look of skin that had burned but never quite healed. Holding a sign above her head, she seemed impervious to the catcalls and whistles that followed her like a lovesick teen. She was a professional, this one. Probably one of the last left, in fact.

Bruno had made his entrance a little early, so he flexed his muscles, jogged in place, and halfheartedly punched at the air. His eyes scanned the room, taking everything in at a glance. It was a learned response not limited to this specific place and event: everywhere he went, he methodically took the same precautions. Every step. Every moment of what passed for his miserable little life. Constant vigilance and hyperawareness were the name of the game, and he planned to win for as long as he could.

The sumo wrestler, Bruno noticed, hadn't lasted long. A couple of lanky guys were busy scrubbing his blood from the floor while a third speared chunks of flesh with a tool that once picked litter from a park. What was left of the big guy was carried out on a covered stretcher, two extra men on each side to accommodate the weight. One massive arm had slipped out from beneath the red-splotched sheet and its finger pointed at the ground, almost as though it were purposefully marking its path with the perforated trail of blood that dripped from the meaty hand.

Where the hell did they find a sumo wrestler, anyway?

Bruno glanced to his right, where a man with a ring of shoulder-length brown hair surrounding a bald dome was jostled by a crowd of people. Scribbling furiously in his spiral ring notebook, the man scratched out code that was as indecipherable to most as hieroglyphs, but the glint of intelligence in his dark eyes was enough to let people know he wasn't fucking around. He knew each name, each bet, and could be counted on not to squelch. This earned him the closest thing to trust this world had to offer. His goons snatched outstretched cans of food from the eager hands that surrounded him. In return, they received a scrap of paper and a smile from the boss himself.

"Say, Smitty!" Bruno shouted through the controlled chaos of the crowd, "where'd they find a sumo?"

Smitty's eyes flitted from the notebook just long enough to make contact. He quickly resumed writing, his pencil worn down to a nub while scratching furiously across the paper. "Dunno, champ. The poor fat fuck didn't stand a chance, though. Put on a good show with the stompin' and throwing of the sand and all. But when the bell rang, he was bleedin' before the sound had a chance to fade."

Bruno sniffed once and rolled his head in circles, limbering his neck. "Better show from me," he promised. "Main event, baby."

"We'll see about that. Ten to one against. Death's the ultimate bad ass, friend, and a lot of folks think your number's just about up."

"Shit…un-*fucking*-defeated, here." The banter was a bad rendition of the roles they both played, lacking the warm tones of honest conversation. Still, Bruno felt a little silly. It was obvious to anyone with a working pair of eyes that he'd never lost a fight. He was, after all, still alive. "And planning to keep it that way, too. Bite free since '23, mother fucker."

The scarred beauty leaned her placard against a table and took up a silver hammer, which she then struck back and forth between two of the cage's bars. The jangling sound was optimistically called "the bell," and just like that, it was go time.

Entering the cage through a door which was locked behind him, Bruno held his hands in the air, forming the shape of a V. There was no referee to have a quick word with, no meeting in the center of the ring before going to respective corners. The age of niceties had been left behind, its staunch tenacity toward decorum abandoned as if it were just another body littering the streets.

When a surge of excitement rippled through the audience and their cheers reached deafening levels, he knew his opponent was being escorted to the cage. Two biker types steered Bruno's adversary toward the ring, each one clutching a long rod that ended with a loop of rope. One of these loops pinned his arms to his side and the other encircled his waste, acting as a rudder. In a real fight, he would have been a featherweight, and pitting him against a man of Bruno's stature was almost unheard of. But it wasn't exactly size that mattered in this match. With a black sack over his head, he thrashed and fought violently against the restraints, jilting and staggering the burly handlers, who constantly shouted back and forth as they made corrections to the trajectory.

The door on the other side of the ring had a square hole welded out of its center, and this allowed the rods to bridge the gap between killing floor and safety as the padlock snapped shut. The thugs yanked Bruno's opponent backward so hard that the entire cage shook and another man's arm snaked through the bars, clutching the black sack as he waited for the agreed-upon signal. In unison, they nodded and the ropes were released as if magically severed, the bag snatched from the fighter's head.

Thinning red hair stuck out in tufts, almost as if he'd just stumbled out of bed, and his yellowed teeth gnashed at the air. He almost looked normal, but it was the little things that gave his condition away. The lack of contraction in his dilated pupils. The creepy stillness of expression that was still able to send shivers down Bruno's spine. The flesh was both pasty and waxen at the same time with shadows adding depth to sunken cheeks-it was a look the rest of the world knew too well. A silver band dangled from one nipple and blood from a gunshot wound still matted the curly hair on his chest. The bastard couldn't have been more than twenty minutes dead, which meant he would still be fast and cagey. Bruno never dared to question how the organizers found such fresh corpses.

Even if he'd had the inclination to form such questions, he didn't have the time. Before the rods were completely withdrawn, the thing sprinted across the ring. Its outstretched arms reached toward Bruno with fingers curled into talon-like hooks, and the explosive cheer from the crowd was pushed to the periphery. With his concentration focused and the audience muted to background noise, Bruno darted in with his gloves held before his face.

The first jab smacked into the thing's jaw with a flat smack, and the force spun the creature around as if the floor had slipped beneath its feet. Not quite falling, the corpse sprang forward before centrifugal force finished its business. But Bruno was ready for that as well. A roundhouse to the side of the thing's face knocked it off course and its body tumbled across the floor.

This was it. *The* moment. Only when facing death did Bruno feel most alive. His heart thumped adrenaline through a body that felt as tough and efficient as an old world machine: keenly aware of every muscle, every twitch or spasm, with his feet shuffling their intricate dance and beads of sweet beginning to cool his brow.

There were no rounds in this fight, no brief respites from combat where he could catch his breath and spit blood into a bucket. The dead were relentless in their single-minded pursuit, oblivious to pain or fatigue. They kept coming at their prey time and time again, wearing them down with persistence until superior muscle tone no longer held sway. Only one could remain: kill or be killed, after all, was the law of this post-apocalyptic jungle. Besides, the audience had paid for a show and his share of the prize would make him rich.

In this graveyard of a world, aluminum was the new gold. A single can of pork and beans would net him a good time with any of the food whores down by the tracks. Ten tins of sardines would pay his monthly protection to Boss Nash, and there would still be plenty left over. In a land where the dead scoured the ruins for the slightest signs of the living, this was what passed for a playboy lifestyle. And it suited Bruno just fine.

The zombie was on its feet again, lurching toward with its entire torso leaning forward. Lacking that spark of life, eyes that were as dusty and emotionless as marbles stared unblinkingly at the intended target. Anxious to keep the initiative in his favor, Bruno moved in like a striking snake. So close to the damn thing that he caught whiffs of its recently voided bowels, he realized his mistake. The zombie had been moving a little more quickly than he realized and he'd overcompensated. He was close enough for the thing's fingernails to rake across his vinyl gloves.

An uppercut to the face only succeeded in piercing the thing's top lip with a broken tooth. A flurry of jabs cracked ribs like twigs, yet the zombie remained unfazed. With its fingers now entangled in the laces, it yanked the glove toward its face. Teeth ripped through the outer shell and tore strands of white stuffing from the hole, which the zombie then released with a shake of the head.

All of Bruno's skills and training deserted him. The grace was gone from his savage dance and he'd regressed to nothing more than a street fighter. His blows were uncoordinated and sloppy, thrown from his weak arm with no real planning or strategy, and bounced ineffectually off the zombie's head as it ripped more stuffing from the glove.

The roar of the crowd was thrown back into sharp focus: shouts and stomps, glass bottles of moonshine shattering against the walls, some indecipherable chant rising and falling like a wave in the turbulent ocean of noise. Bruno's throat felt raw and tight as his own scream added to the din, as he kicked with quick thrusts of his legs in hopes of clipping the creature at the knees. The walking corpse had eaten so far into the glove that Bruno felt its chin scissoring over the thin layer of batting, pulling away the only barrier between those teeth and soft, living flesh, like a savage wolf devouring a fresh kill. The thing's hands were totally ensnared in the boxing glove's laces, and it was impossible for Bruno to pull away. The creature's hands flopped like fish that had been thrown into a cat's cradle, pulling and stretching until the glove no longer fit as snugly as it once had.

The hundreds of feet stomping against the bleachers had picked up a rhythm now: two quick stomps followed by a single hand clap. For one insane second, Bruno actually expected the crowd to launch into the chorus of *We Will Rock You*, but then other thoughts pinged through his mind like ricocheting bullets, obliterating one another before they had a chance to fully form. Instead of reason there were only flashing bursts of emotion: fear, intense sadness, a nameless longing for something he would never know...but mostly remorse.

Like a dirty fighter, regret hits you when you're not looking. It lurks in the darkness, awaiting its time to pounce before fading back into the shadows. Sensing weakness, the regret didn't strike and run this time. It stood its ground and shredded the remaining strands of self-respect as thoroughly as the zombie did his glove.

Bruno's hand wiggled like a loose tooth in a socket as he struggled to free himself. He felt the silk lining sliding over his knuckle and cool air rush in through the gnawed hole. The zombie plunged its face in again, and with the protection of the glove no longer an issue, it could see the pink flesh of fingers, and the sight seemed to throw it into a frenzy. Its hand writhed in the tangle of laces, pushing and pulling, demanding to be freed. Nothing mattered but the feast, and the audience ate up every second of it as their voices rose into a thunderous din.

Just as the undead bastard sank its face into the hole, Bruno's hand popped free, leaving the abomination to snap at empty air. Still operating on pure survival instinct, he immediately launched into a flurry of punches. His taped knuckles slammed into the creature's face so hard that a fracture-like pain flared in his middle finger. Again and again, jack rabbit fast, ignoring the shock of sudden impact: Bruno was a single-fisted juggernaut whose wild eyes told a story as old as the dinosaurs. Here was life and death splayed out for all to see. Here was the endless struggle for dominance in an uncaring world. It was the type of moment where you could be wholly and completely reborn...or die.

Bruno skirted backward, extending his reach as the zombie lunged, and struck with his gloved hand. His frenzy had been tamed now and each hit was more solid than the last. The zombie's nose broke with a sharp crack and the jagged bone forced its way through the skin in a bloodless explosion of meat. Teeth plinked like porcelain against the polished, wood floor, and Bruno continued his barrage.

The zombie lunged again, but the sweat-drenched prizefighter was ready. He spun away just before the collision, his unfettered hand clutching the thing's hair as his body swung around and crashed into the back of the creature. With momentum working to his advantage, Bruno drove the monster forward, and the thing's head crashed into the unforgiving bars of the cage. Bashed repeatedly against the steel, the creature's forehead took on a dented look, as if bone were caving in just below the surface. And yet, Bruno continued his assault long after the thing's limbs went limp. He knew it was "true dead," as they called it in the business, but found himself powerless to stop. His body was a killing machine that, once revved up, had to be given time to power down.

By the time he allowed the zombie's body to crumple to the floor, the doors to the cage were unlocked. The crowd was going wild with applause and the scarred bikini model carried a large bowl of canned goods as if it were an offering to the gods. The bowl was mostly symbolic. The food within it would definitely be included in his prize, but the true wealth of the purse was so great the woman would have been crushed beneath it.

He hadn't needed Smitty to tell him the odds. He knew that nobody really expected him to live. A few private bets placed on the side had netted him a fortune in food. He would eat for weeks without even once considering rationing, and would have his pick of the higher-class food whores instead of settling for diseased guttersnipes. His life was about to become very, very good.

Bruno held his hands aloft and bounced across the floor as he played to the crowd. There were more than a handful of boos scattered among the applause, but you always had that. The only thing that mattered was Bruno would be eating well and they would not.

Pausing to wink at the ring girl, Bruno noticed his hand and felt as though he'd taken a sucker punch to the groin. Bile stung the back of his throat and his breath caught on the bitter flood of acid, becoming nothing more than a sharp gasp with no follow up.

His heart was a runaway locomotive and the blood surging through his veins felt cold. He stared at the back of his bare hand as the broad smile melted and his face drained of color.

He recalled landing that first punch after freeing himself from the glove: there'd been a flash of pain, what he'd suspected to be a hairline fracture. But, no. There it was, a jagged little break in the skin, nothing more than a scrape really. In another world, in another time, it would have meant nothing, but in the wastelands there was no word for inconsequential. Even something as small as the flap of bloodstained skin carried grave consequences. In the trade, it was known as *fighter's bite* and not to be taken lightly. Regardless of whether you'd been chewed on like a soup bone or just nicked your knuckle while landing a punch, the results were the same.

Bruno would never live to enjoy his food. He'd never fuck again. In his profession, death was a career path, and he thought he'd been ready for it. He really did. He'd always sworn he'd never be one of *those* assholes: the ones who tried to hide a wound, who went about their business in an exaggerated manner, almost as if they were calling attention to the fact that everything was normal. But when faced with infection, priorities change without debate.

Lifting his tattered glove as if it were the severed head of an enemy, Bruno turned in a slow circle and played the part of victorious champion. Wriggling his hand into its confines, he forced a smile. His fighter's bite was now hidden, but how long did he have left? Fifteen minutes? Half an hour? Even less if anyone noticed that his sweat continued streaming long after he should have cooled down. Either way, he'd be dead before the fires in the burning barrels gutted out.

But those were *his* moments, damn it, and he planned on savoring every second he had left. And who knew?

Once that last breath rattled his soul free and his muscles twitched with the semblance of life, maybe Boss Nash would allow him to continue his career.

ABOUT THE WRITERS

Rocky Alexander currently resides in North Carolina, where he spends his time as a horror fiction writer and boxing coach. He takes comfort in the knowledge that, after having survived 80's hair bands, the end of the world will seem like a piece of cake.

Vincenzo Bilof is an educator who lives in Detroit, Michigan. He was awarded the "2011 Literary Achievement Award" by SNM Horror Magazine after publishing 8 consecutive stories for their monthly contests. His work appears in the anthologies "Bonded by Blood: Scarlet Sunset" by SNM Publishing, "Frightmares" by Dark Moon Books, and "Book of the Dead 6" by Living Dead Press. His horror stories also appear in 6 anthologies from Open Casket Press, including "Gnomes of the Dead" and "Mutant Apocalypse." The story appearing in Zombie Tales titled "Hero's End" features the protagonist, Lenin, from Vincenzo's zombie-apocalypse novel "Under a Red Sun," forthcoming from OCP.

Daniel Ciesielski is a native of Macomb, Michigan. His interests include reading and writing fantasy novels. He is currently working on the novel, "Death in Palm of My Hand."

Alyn Day is an active member of the New England Horror Writers living outside of Boston, MA. She is an avid horror enthusiast with an inclination towards zombies. Publications include So Long and Thanks for All the Brains, Daily Frights 2012, "Women of the Living Dead," and "Zombie Tales." Upcoming works include "Mirror, Mirror," "Daily Frights 2013," and "Here Be Clowns."

Joseph Dumas was raised in Natick, Massachusetts. He's been a zombie/horror enthusiast ever since he was young. Combined with his love for creative writing, he has found himself constantly putting together stories about the undead and other apocalyptic themes. In January 2012, he published his first book entitled "Decay: A Zombie Story" through Open Casket Press. In addition to his writing, he's currently finishing up his degree in English and Education at the University of Mass. He plans to teach elementary school and continue writing on the side.

T. Fox Dunham resides outside of Philadelphia PA. He's published in over fifty international journals and anthologies and was a finalist in the Copper Nickel Annual Short Story Contest for his story, The Lady Comes in the Night. He's currently finishing his first zombie apocalypse novella, Dead Dominion. He's a cancer survivor. His friends call him fox, being his totem animal, and his motto is: Wrecking civilization one story at a time.

Joe Filippone is a fulltime actor and writer currently living in Hollywood, California whose work has appeared in numerous anthologies including "Letters From The Dead," "Baconology," "The Undead That Saved Christmas" and "Thirsty Are The Damned." He is also the author of the books "Real Boys Kiss Boys" (CAPA Nomination YA Fiction), "The Christmas Cottage" and "In The Tarot."

Anthony Giangregorio is the author of 40 novels, almost all of them about zombies, and has edited over 40 anthologies and books. His work has appeared in Dead Science & Metahumans vs. the Undead by Coscomentertainment, Dead Worlds: Undead Stories Volumes 1-7, and Wolves of War by Library of the Living Dead Press. He also has stories in End of Days: An Apocalyptic Anthology Vol. 1-5, the Book of the Dead series Vol. 1-6 by LDP, Zombie Zoology by Severed Press, and two anthologies with Pill Hill Press. He's also the creator of the 10 book action/zombie series titled Deadwater and the apocalyptic series Warriors of the Apocalypse. His action/horror novel Dead Rage is being optioned for a movie at this time. Visit him on Facebook.

Ash Hartwell is living proof that life begins at forty. Since surviving that long he has now had stories published by Static Movement, Living Dead Press and Wicked East Press. He should really be concentrating on writing his first novel now. You can find him on Facebook.

Gabino Iglesias is a writer and journalist currently working on his PhD in journalism. His non-fiction work has appeared in The New York Times, the Austin Post, Business Today magazine, San Antonio magazine and many other publications. His fiction has appeared in Bizarro Central, MicroHorror, El Nuevo Dia and a few anthologies that will be released in 2012, including The Plastic Electric Baby Jesus and other Bizarro Zombie Tales. He lives in Austin, TX.

Jennifer Koehler lives and works in Ohio. Look for her short stories in Post Mortem Press' "Mon Coeur Mort" and Open Casket Press' "Women of the Living Dead."

William Todd Rose writes speculative fiction that lends itself to the dark, and often surreal, realm of the macabre. To date, his full length works include "Shadow of the Woodpile," "Cry Havoc," "Sex in the Time of Zombies," "Shut the F*#K Up and Die!," "Apocalyptic Organ Grinder," "The Dead and Dying" and "The Seven Habits of Highly Infective People." For more information, including links to free fiction, please visit the author online at www.williamtoddrose.com

Timothy Tarkelly is a theater major from Kansas.

Jonathan Templar lives in Cheshire, England. His recent published and soon to be published work includes short stories in Open Casket Press's collection "Dead Christmas" ('Secret Santa'), the shared world anthology "World's Collider" ('Basher'), Smart Rhino's collection "Zippered Flesh" ('Marvin's Angry Angel'), and in Wicked East Press' "Bedtime Stories for Girls," but nobody believes him when he mentions that.
Contact him at www. jonathantemplar.com

DEADLY HUNT

by Mariah Deitrick

When extreme hunt enthusiast, Drake Marshal, began his career as a hired hunter, he had no idea he would one day become the prey. If he had, he never would have found himself running for his life in a zombie-infested jungle.

Will Drake's years of hunting experience be enough to keep him alive? Or will he let his sympathy for others get him killed.

CAVALCADE OF TERROR
A HORROR ANTHOLOGY

Edited by Vincenzo Bilof

Ghosts, monsters and serial killers abound in this collection of horror stories not for the faint of heart, written by both established and up and coming new authors.

In the darkness within us all resides a demon no one can destroy, one that feeds on carnage and mayhem. Though you may try to deny this, you know it's true. Human beings are no more than animals, filled with selfishness, greed and evil intentions.

Will you face your true self or continue hiding in the shadows?

If unsure, then delve into these pages of terror and unlock your innermost fears.

UNDEAD PRESS

UNDEADPRESS.COM

OPEN CASKET PRESS

OPEN CASKET PRESS.COM

THE NEW NAME IN HORROR

9 781611 990492